Four of a Kind

Africa Kirk

Copyright © 2023 by Africa Kirk

All rights reserved. This book or any portion thereof may not be reproduced or transmitted in any form or manner, electronic or mechanical, including photocopying, recording, or by any information storage or retrieval system, without the express written permission of the copyright owner except for the use of brief quotations in a book review or other noncommercial uses permitted by copyright law.

Printed in the United States of America
Library of Congress Control Number: 2023907210
ISBN: Softcover   979-8-88963-400-3
        e-Book   979-8-88963-401-0

Republished by: PageTurner Press and Media LLC
Publication Date: 05/24/2023

To order copies of this book, contact:
PageTurner Press and Media
Phone: 1-888-447-9651
info@pageturner.us
www.pageturner.us

This is dedicated to my family;

I love you all through thick and thin.

Chapter 1

It's been a busy day at the salon. I have been working from one client to the next, nonstop. I've been a beautician for twenty years, working in different salons. I thought about opening my own one day but between my sons' school activities and taking care of Dad, I didn't have the time. I have a high clientele and the money would be better. My husband Patrick is a dentist with his own practice. He was always busy but made time for his family. My boys are both in junior high, straight A students, and stayed out of trouble. One played football and the other basketball. As I rolled my clients' hair, I began thinking about Dad. He has been sick for a long time and is in the hospital. I love him and fear losing him. My family and I live in east Fort Worth, and Dad lived nearby. My two little sisters lived in different states, and I've been taking care of him.

Dad raised us but our mother was never around. I have a faint memory of her, but I was little. I often wondered who she was, if she was alive, or if we had other siblings. I wanted to find her and didn't know how to tell my sisters. I wondered if they had the same thoughts. I wanted to ask Dad, but I never did. He's going through enough, and I didn't want him to stress over her. I would tell my husband, but he would suggest that I ask Dad.

After work, I drove straight to the hospital. Dad was being discharged tomorrow and the doctor wanted to talk to me. Getting him to obey the doctor's orders was a challenge. It drove me crazy, and he could be difficult. My husband helped when he could but doing everything alone was exhausting. I arrived at the hospital and went to Dad's room. He was lying in bed, watching TV. I hugged him and he felt fragile. He lost a lot of weight and looked tired. I wish there was something I could do to take him out of his misery. Dad was a joker and always made us laugh to keep us from worrying about him. It would only work for the moment. I laughed and talked with him while waiting for the doctor. Hopefully, Dad will listen to her this time. His doctor was good, and they developed a friendship. Dad had that way with everyone. People were drawn to his personality and if he ever had an enemy, it was their fault. Dad was cool and laid back, but he had a temper that would send a person running.

"How are you feeling today?"

"I'm doing better." He said. "I'm ready to go home and look at my big screen." I stared at him, and he looked at me like I was crazy. "What?"

"Nothing."

"Don't lie to me, Alexis."

"I'm just worried about you. You look exhausted and I don't want to lose you."

He turned off the TV and sat up in the bed. "Alexis, you are not going to lose me." He said. "I've been a diabetic most of your lives, I'm used to this. I've been through this before and I'm still here. I want you and your sisters to do something for me."

"Anything."

"Stop worrying about me." He said.

I looked at him and smiled. "Okay."

"Good evening, Alexis." Dad's doctor said, walking in.

"Hey Roslyn."

"How are you feeling Morris?"

"I'm good."

Roslyn opened her chart. "We're discharging you tomorrow at noon. We're prescribing you more medicine for your blood pressure. Morris, you have to change your diet."

"I will." After discussing Dad's health, Roslyn left.

"I'm going to get some sleep." Dad said, getting comfortable. "You can either stay and watch or go home."

"Okay Dad, good night. I'll see you tomorrow. I love you."

"Love you too. Shut the door." I laughed and closed the door behind me.

As I was walking towards the elevator, Roslyn stopped me. "Alexis, can I talk to you for a moment?"

"Sure, what's wrong?"

"I didn't want to say this in front of your dad but, he must watch his diet. His sugar went up so high the other night, I thought he was going to go into a diabetic coma. When I told him, he became very defensive. Maybe he'll listen if he hears it from you."

My heart raced. "Thanks Roslyn."

I parked in my garage and went inside. My husband and our sons were in the family room, playing video games. I walked in the kitchen and Patrick followed me. "How is your dad?" He asked.

"He's okay. He goes home tomorrow, and Roslyn is prescribing him *more* medicine for his blood pressure."

"Are you okay?" He asked. "It looks like something else is on your mind."

"Roslyn stopped me as I was walking towards the elevator. She told me that his sugar went up so high the other night that she thought he was going to go into a diabetic coma."

Patrick's mouth dropped and he moved closer to me and wrapped his masculine arms around me. "I'm sorry, baby."

"Don't be. Telling my dad to stay away from sweets is like telling a child they can't have candy. He spices up everything he eats, and his blood pressure is constantly going up. I'm stressed and I have no help."

"Alexis, don't stress yourself out." He said. "Just relax and talk to him."

"I tried. He says okay and the minute I leave he does the opposite. Jaz and Dina aren't here to help. I'm just frustrated."

"I understand your frustration but, if you need help, ask your sisters. I'm here too."

"Dina never has a free moment and Jaz is busy with her husband and son."

Patrick lifted my head and kissed me. "You have me, and I don't mind helping you, baby. Just let me know." I nodded. "What's for dinner?"

"Pizza."

He paused and laughed. "I could have ordered that."

"I'm sorry, I should have called you."

"That's okay, baby. I'm going to beat Junior in this game."

Dad and I arrived at his house from the hospital. He was glad to be home and so was I. He walked straight to the den and sat in his recliner chair. "Comfortable?"

"Very." He said. "I missed my chair more than I missed y'all."

"Okay Dad, I'm about to leave. Do you need anything?"

"Alexis, my legs aren't broken, and I have my truck and my new car. I'm fine."

Just before he went in the hospital, he bought a new white Cadillac CT6. It was *gorgeous*. He had his old truck for over a decade, it was in mint condition, and a lot of people have tried to buy it from him. Dad had a lot of money but never splurged and had been living in the same house since we were in junior high. He mentioned renovating it but never started. I made Dad promise me that he will watch his diet and to take his medicine. Hopefully he will keep his promise.

I was glad he was home before the Thanksgiving holidays. My sisters will be in town and we're cooking at Dad's house. I can't wait to see them and my nephew. I arrived at work and one of my classmates from high school walked in. Traci and I always stayed in touch, and she is very successful. We were more than best friends. Patrick and her husband are brothers. Traci and her husband were entrepreneurs, and she owned a restaurant at a lake. It was the hottest restaurant throughout the state, and she was an amazing cook. Her parents owned a blues club that had been running for years. Dad and Uncle Ernest went a lot. Patrick and I checked it out before and loved it. Traci was tall like me, had long coarse hair, beautiful dark skin, green eyes, and wasn't afraid to live. She and her husband had eight children and they live in a massive house in the suburbs. Traci knew Dad as well. He treated all of my friends like they were his children.

I finished styling Traci's hair, and she invited me to a late lunch to catch up. We went to a nearby diner and ordered our meals. "So, how is everything going?" She asked.

"Everything is okay. Just working and taking care of my dad and my family."

"How is Mr. Morris?"

"He's doing better. He was released from the hospital earlier and I took him home before I got to the salon."

"I'm sorry, Alexis." She said. "Your dad was always like a father to me and Shonda."

"How is Shonda?"

"She's doing well. She and my brother are still happily married."

"The women loved your brother." She laughed. Traci nearly had to fight some of the women for acting crazy behind her big brother. "How is Harold?

"He's doing well. How are Jaz and Dina?"

"They are good. They will be here for Thanksgiving."

"We'll be selling deep fried turkeys. I'll have two for you." After talking and catching up, Traci went back to work, and I went back to the salon.

Later, business slowed down, and I was tired, but the money was good. I checked on Dad, and he had just woken up from a nap. He seemed energized and back to himself. I called my sisters and they confirmed they were still coming for Thanksgiving next month. But they wanted to see Dad before then after him being in the hospital. After work, I left.

It was the end of October, and it was getting chilly. I loved fall and thought about buying fall harvest decorations. I went home and Patrick had dinner ready, and the boys were doing their homework. We ate and the boys cleaned the kitchen. I decided to sit on the covered patio and wrapped myself in my throw blanket. I gazed into the sunset trying to clear my mind, taking deep breaths. "Mind if I join you?" Patrick asked, walking out.

"Not at all." He wrapped his arms around me, and we kissed. "The sunset is beautiful."

"Yes, it is. Are you okay?"

"I'm okay. How was your day?" Patrick and I talked and watched the sunset.

Jaz

Chapter 2

My son and I are flying to Texas tomorrow. He will be staying with his dad while I visit my big sister Alexis and Daddy. I missed him and wanted to check on him after hearing that he almost went into a diabetic coma. There are times when I get homesick but, my husband Carlin would always find a way to cheer me up. Daddy liked him but Alexis cannot stand him.

I met Carlin in college and after we graduated, I flew home and ran into my son's dad, my high school sweetheart, Kel. I got pregnant and lived with him for a while. I was later offered a job in North Carolina and went for it. Daddy encouraged me to follow my dreams and MJ and I moved here. We were living in a crappy apartment, and I ran into Carlin again. Carlin was very handsome and looked like he modeled for *GQ Magazine*. He was six-foot-two, had an athletic build, a well-groomed beard, light-skinned, and was the corporate kind of guy. In my day, we called his type, *pretty boys*. We talked, began dating, and I later introduced him to my son. He was taking over his dad's auto dealerships in North Carolina and asked me to marry him. I accepted. My family thought I was moving too fast, especially Alexis. I think it was because she didn't like Carlin. Carlin and I had a courthouse wedding and spent our honeymoon in Japan. I didn't know how MJ's dad felt when he received the news about me getting married but, I didn't care. I wanted to be with Kel, but he was busy being a player and pushed me away. I was hurt but refused to wait for him.

Carlin's dad owned a major dealership here in North Carolina and he left it to Carlin when he died. I love wine and we started a vineyard here in Charlotte and opened stores throughout North Carolina and surrounding states. Carlin was busy with the dealership, and I ran the vineyard and stores. I had visions of expanding but, Carlin cared more about the dealership. He already lived in our house – a massive two-story with four bedrooms, a billiard room, a pool, and a six-car garage. It was contemporary, and he shared it with me and MJ. I often thought about Kel at that time but, I was happy here with Carlin, doing something that I always wanted to do – run a business. Carlin met Kel a few times and the tension was heavy. Kel wasn't happy but, I felt he was jealous. Carlin took care of MJ, but MJ always had a strong relationship with his dad, although he was back home in Texas. Kel always made time for our son and would talk to him all hours of the night if he had too.

There was no doubt that Carlin didn't like Kel. Whenever it came to MJ going to see his dad, Carlin had something smart to say, and it eventually got on my nerves.

Carlin was lying in bed on his laptop, and I was packing. He was always working and only gave me attention when I was flying back home. I had my hair braided yesterday and he didn't say anything. "Are you excited about seeing Kel?" Carlin asked, being sarcastic.

"Honey don't start. I'm going to help Alexis with my dad. He just got out of the hospital, and she needs a break. MJ wants to stay with his dad and I'm letting him."

The doorbell rang and he went to answer it while I continued packing. "Hey Jaz!" Denise said, walking in the room.

Denise and I went to college together and we've been friends ever since. She was the only person other than family I would let walk freely into my bedroom. "Hey Denise, how are you?"

"I'm great." She said, sitting on the bed. "I love your braids!"

"Thank you! I had it done yesterday."

"I see you're packing for Texas."

"Yes, I'm giving my sister a break for the weekend and MJ is staying with his dad."

She and I chatted for a while, and she got ready to leave.

"I was just passing through and thought I'd stop by. Call me when you get back." She left and I finished packing.

I went upstairs to check on MJ. I peeked in his bedroom, and he was fast asleep with the TV on. I turned it off, kissed him on the cheek, and walked out. I went downstairs and Carlin sat our luggage in the foyer. "Is he asleep?" He asked.

"Yes, I'm about to crash too."

He wrapped his arms around me as we walked to our bedroom. We were all over each other. The only time Carlin showed me any affection was when I was going to Texas. Genuine or not, I cherished it.

Me and MJ landed in Texas and found Alexis. We hugged each other and walked to her car. I was so happy to see her. Alexis was nurturing and whenever we were around each other, I felt calm and relieved. She was the strong one of the three of us, and I don't know how she holds it together. Every time I see her, she has a new look. She was wearing jeans, a fitted sweater, and designer winter boots. Alexis had long hair, down her back. She didn't have a fancy hairstyle this time. It was in a ponytail, but she looked flawless. Her makeup was always pretty and so was her jewelry. Everyone loved Alexis' chic and trendy style. We arrived at Daddy's house and walked inside. "Dad?" Alexis called.

Daddy walked in the living room, and I ran to hug him. He felt small and fragile. "Hi Daddy, how are you?"

"I'm doing good." He said, looking at me. "How about you?"

"I'm doing good."

"How is my grandson?" Daddy played with MJ, and I stood there looking at how much weight Daddy lost. Alexis and I looked at each other. "Well, put your bags in the bedroom and sit down." He said.

We visited for a while and Alexis went back to work. I called Kel to let him know I was dropping MJ off. Daddy loaned me his truck and we left. We arrived at Kel's house, and I became nervous. He lived in a nice house in southwest Fort Worth and had been living here for years. I grabbed MJ's bags out of the truck and rang the doorbell. "What's up, Jaz?" Kel's brother asked, opening the door.

"Hey Donnie, how are you?"

"I'm doing good, how are you?" He asked, hugging me.

We walked inside and sat in the living room. Kel kept a clean house, and he was organized. Donnie played with MJ, and I waited. "Where is Kel?"

"He's in the shower." For some reason, I was more nervous.

It's been a while since our last visit, and I would always get butterflies whenever it came to seeing Kel. I walked around the living room and looked at the pictures he had on his glass curios. On one of the shelves was a picture of us when I was two months pregnant with MJ. It brought back memories when we used to go out together and travel. His house was a bachelor's pad; black leather furniture, big screen TV, surround sound, video games, *and* Kel can cook. I wish he and Carlin could get along. MJ liked Carlin and felt comfortable around him. But the minute I mention his dad, he would drop everything.

"Well, well, well." I jumped when I heard Kel's deep voice. My heart was skipping beats when I saw him. He was wearing sweatpants, a t-shirt, and socks. Kel was *so* fine and very easy on the eyes. He was six-foot-five, stocky but athletic, dark chocolate skin, had a beard and mustache, chestnut brown eyes, and the way he looked at me made me weak. He was a casual guy, would never fit in the corporate world, he made a t-shirt and jeans look expensive, always smelled good, and had the sexiest deep raspy voice. He was a barber and made a lot of money. "How are you, Mrs. Jazmine *Lawrence*?" I hated the way he said my married name. "You look good."

"Thanks. So do you, *Markell Clark*."

He hugged me and Donnie was watching our every move. MJ ran to him, and they played. I stood there watching them, wishing that MJ could be around him more. "Come on MJ." Donnie said. "Let's go to the back so you can get settled."

"Bye MJ. Be good."

"Bye Momma." He said, waving.

Kel was standing there, staring at me. He had that sexy look in his eyes, and it made my heart race. "So, how have you been?" He asked.

"I've been good. How about you?"

"I've been alright. I just work and come home."

"How is your mom?"

"She's fine. She still asks about you after all this time."

Ms. Sandy was like a mother to me. She always told Kel that I was her favorite. "How about Tonya?"

"She's fine, still putting up with Donnie." He said, sitting on the sofa. "You know, I got a little jealous when they got married."

I sat next to him. "Why?"

"It doesn't matter."

"Then why did you say it?"

"I don't know. I guess I got caught up in the moment."

Curiosity was killing me. "What were you going to say, Kel?"

"We could have been married." He finally said.

I paused. "You weren't ready, and I wasn't going to wait for you."

"Are you happy?" He asked, looking me in my eyes.

"I have to go." I stood and walked towards the door. "I'll be here Sunday afternoon."

He followed me and stopped me. "You didn't answer my question. Are you happy?"

"Bye Kel." I left.

I was in a daze, driving back to Daddy's house. My mind was going in different directions and Carlin called. He was checking in and we talked until I arrived at Daddy's house. I napped most of the afternoon, and Daddy was watching TV when I woke up. I talked with him for a while and in the middle of our conversation, I began thinking about Kel. "Jaz, what are you thinking about?" I told him about me and Kel's conversation and the question I avoided. "You know what Jaz, I like Carlin." He said. "He's nice, a hard worker, and a great provider. You got married at the courthouse and you looked happy. Now, don't take this the wrong way but, there is something about Carlin that bothers me."

Daddy's suspicions were always spot on. "What do you think it is?"

"I don't know. But you will find out and I hope your heart doesn't get broken." I thought about what he said but, Carlin wouldn't hurt me. "I know you love your husband, and he loves you but, whenever Kel is around, you glow. Carlin notices and gets jealous."

"He knows I would never cheat on him."

"But do you believe that he would never cheat on you?" Daddy asked.

Later that night, I went to Patrick and Alexis' house. I loved their house. It was cozy and warm for a big single-story house. I joined them for dinner and helped Alexis wash the dishes. I told her about my conversations with Daddy and Kel. "I'm telling you Jaz, I don't trust Carlin." She said. "He's nice and all but, there is something sneaky about him."

The doorbell rang and Alexis rushed to the door. I looked up and saw my baby sister and ran to her. "Dina! How are you?"

"Hey Jaz!" Dina said. "I'm doing good. How are you?"

"I'm fine."

"Let's sit and chat."

We laughed and talked, and I forgot how loud Dina could be. When I was with Kel, we all were close. People asked about Dina the most. She was the bookworm and lived in New York. She was so beautiful and the tallest of me and Alexis. Dina was six-feet tall, slim, but had curves, and was all legs. Her thick jet-black hair was down her back, she had a baby face, and was light skinned. Like Alexis, she could dress, but was sporty. She loved sneakers, jeans, and ball caps. But when she was working, she was in designer suits. I missed this – laughing, and talking with my sisters, and Daddy. Then I thought about Carlin and wondered if he was the cause of me not being around them. Later, Dina and I left. She was staying with Daddy, and he talked to us about his health and gave us advice on life and relationships. It was like old times.

It's Sunday morning and I was packing my bags to go back home today. Dina was staying for a week. I wish I could stay longer. I enjoyed the weekend and Alexis was able to relax. I wasn't ready to leave but, I wanted my husband, and MJ had school tomorrow. Yesterday, I hung out with my sisters and my best friend Tonya. Tonya was married to Kel's brother, and we used to hang out all the time when I was still living in Texas. I missed her and we planned to stay in touch. Back in high school, it was me, Tonya, and Juanita. I was the party animal, Tonya was loud and sassy, and Juanita was the fighter. I plan to catch up with them on the next visit.

I borrowed Daddy's truck to pick up MJ, and once again, I was nervous. I then began to cry, for some reason. I felt lonely and miserable at the same time. I have a sick dad and a jealous husband who seemed too busy to spend quality time with me. I guess I'm just homesick.

I arrived at Kel's house and rang the doorbell. "Hey, come on in." He said, opening the door.

"Is he ready?"

"I'll get him." Kel had MJ's bags packed and I sat on the sofa, waiting for them.

They walked in the living room and MJ looked sad. "You ready to go, MJ?"

He nodded and began to cry. Kel sat down and MJ stood before him. "Son, what did I tell you?" He asked him. "Don't cry. Whenever you want to talk to me, call. I don't care if it's in the middle of the night, okay?"

MJ nodded and hugged his dad. My heart dropped and I wish there was a way that I can make this situation better. "Well, we better get going." I walked towards the door. "Come on MJ."

"When will you be back?" Kel asked.

"The week of Thanksgiving. How about MJ spend Thanksgiving with you and your family?"

Kel's face lit up. "That's cool with me." He said. "My mom was happy to see him too."

"Tell her I said hello."

"I will. You two better go."

"Alright. I'll have him call you when we get home." MJ hugged Kel again and we left.

We arrived at Daddy's house and Alexis was there to take us to the airport. I hugged Daddy and Dina for a long time, and we left. Alexis walked us to our tunnel at the airport and we said our goodbyes. I hugged Alexis and I was starting to get emotional. I blamed it on missing Daddy.

We landed in Charlotte and had a car take us home. As I suspected, Carlin wasn't home. I wanted to come home and see my husband but, he wasn't here. I had MJ call his dad and sent him upstairs to get settled. I went to unpack and took a shower. I got comfortable and checked on MJ. He was tired and I could tell he was missing his dad. I called Daddy and talked with him for a while. Later, MJ and I ate, and he got ready for school. Carlin was still gone. I poured myself a glass of wine and relaxed in the family room. I thought about everything and began to wonder what direction my life was going.

Chapter 3

It has been a busy day at the office, and I was on my way home. Once I arrived in Malibu from the L.A. traffic, I let my windows down and enjoyed the breeze off the ocean as it blew through my hair. My husband Reggie and I own a real estate company, *Mitchell Realtors*. Momma helped us start our business after we got married. Reggie and I are high school sweethearts. We've been married for eleven years, and we have one daughter, Yolanda. I want more children but with our schedules, we wouldn't have time, and we traveled often. I'm in my thirties so, there was still time. Yolanda was ten and needed another sibling. I admit that she was spoiled and got her sassy ways from me.

I was spoiled too. Momma raised me and I never knew my dad. I always thought about finding him but never had the courage to ask Momma about him. I would often wonder if I was an only child or if he was still alive. He must be tall because Momma is short. I didn't get my height from her. It would be cool if I had other siblings.

I parked in the garage at our Malibu home and went inside. Reggie and Yolanda were watching TV in the family room. "Hey, you two."

"Hi Momma!" Yolanda ran to me and hugged me.

I sent her to her room to do her homework and Reggie walked towards me. "How was your day, baby?" He asked, hugging me.

"It was long. We had a lot of people calling about that house in Beverly Hills."

"Well, hopefully we will close." He said. "It's a bidding war."

We sat on the sofa and talked more about work. "Also, one of us will have to go to Wisconsin to close the house that's on the hill."

"Oh yeah."

"The family wants to meet us but, I told her that only one of us can go."

"I'll go and don't forget about the business dinner tonight." He said.

I had forgotten all about it. It was a formal networking event. "We better get ready. Can Lisa watch Yolanda?"

"I already called her. She said she would."

I went upstairs and had Yolanda pack her bags to stay at Lisa's house for the night. Lisa's daughter and Yolanda were best friend, and classmates. Lisa and her husband became good friends of me and Reggie.

Reggie wore his black designer tuxedo, and he looked sharp. I took a shower, styled my hair, and applied my makeup. We both were rushing. I put on my black Chanel dress and diamonds. "Is Yolanda ready?" Reggie asked, putting on his Rolex.

"Yes, she's in the family room, waiting on us."

"Which car are we taking?"

"The Bentayga." We rushed out the door.

The event was nice, and we met a lot of people. The party was still going when we left. I was sore and exhausted from dancing. All I wanted to do was crawl in the bed and go to sleep. We walked inside and went straight to the bedroom. "That was nice."

"Yes." He said. "That one was better than last year's event."

We changed clothes and laid in the bed. "Reggie, I know this is random but, I want to find my dad." He turned to me. "I've been thinking about it for a while, and I decided to go for it."

"You know I have your back but, you will have to start with your mom."

"I know and I will talk to her about that. I could have siblings, nieces, and nephews. Yolanda could have someone to play with."

"Ask your mom, baby." Reggie and I lied in bed in each other's arms, talking.

Finding my dad has been on my mind but I didn't know how to bring it up to Momma. She never mentioned him, and I never asked. I've had dreams about him but couldn't see his face. I remember hearing other people but didn't know who they were. Maybe they were my siblings. If I have siblings, why didn't Momma mention them?

I grew up as an only child and I admit that I was spoiled. But Momma whooped me and kept me in line. She traveled a lot on business, and I spent more time with my babysitter. When I started high school, she would leave me home alone. Reggie and I were friends at the time, we hung out, and later started dating. I didn't have many friends in high school because I was known as the *rich girl* and was a brat. I hated that title, and I lost touch with the few friends I had after we graduated high school. I remember going to school and seeing other students getting dropped off and picked up by their fathers but, I was picked up and dropped off by the babysitter. Momma rarely took me to school. I have so many unanswered questions and planned to talk to Momma about my dad.

I arrived at Lisa's house to pick up Yolanda. Lisa and I sat in her breakfast room and talked over a cup of coffee.

Lisa was my best friend and we met in college. We never lost touch and one thing about her was that she didn't sugarcoat anything. She was that friend who would tell you like it is out of love. Lisa was the sibling I never had. "What's going on with you?" She asked.

"Just work. I talked to Reggie last night about me finding my dad."

"Have you talked to Miss. Victoria?"

"Not yet. I can never bring myself to ask her about him. I don't know why."

"I think you should." She suggested. "Just ask her where he is or tell her you want to find him."

"I will. Lisa, what if I have other siblings? Why would my mom keep them from me?"

"Don't jump to conclusions, Yvette. Start with asking her about your dad and go from there. If you do have siblings, question your mom about them, then. You have the right to know."

"You're right. Reggie suggested I talk to my mom too. Yolanda could have cousins."

"You should ask her, soon." She said. "We have six weeks left before the new year. Don't hold it off any longer."

Lisa was right. I've wasted enough time. I want to find my dad and that's my goal. "Do y'all have any plans for Thanksgiving?"

"We're going to my in-law's house. What about y'all?"

"We're going to Reggie's parents' house. We'll be hosting Christmas. Also, Reggie and I are having a big New Year's Eve party at the house. Kids are welcome too."

"We'll be there." Yolanda and I left.

Yolanda went back to sleep, and Reggie and I were sitting on the deck, talking about me finding my dad and the upcoming holiday plans. It was cloudy and the breeze felt good from the ocean. I watched the waves hit the beach and the phone rang and startled me. "Hello?"

"Hey Yvette."

"Hi Momma, how are you?"

"I'm fine. How was the event last night?"

"It was better than last year's party. Me and Reggie are both sore from dancing."

"Where is my granddaughter?" She asked.

"She's asleep. She spent the night at Lisa's house, and I picked her up earlier. Lisa told me that they were up late, watching movies."

"Sounds like she had fun. I was calling to let you know that I will be in town tomorrow. I wanted to see Yolanda."

"Okay, we'll see you then." I still couldn't bring myself to ask Momma about my dad.

Later, the sun peeked through the clouds. Yolanda came running down the stairs, in her little swimsuit, and ran out the patio door. I looked and she jumped into the pool. "Did you see your daughter?"

Yolanda was looking at us, laughing. "I forgot I promised her a swim." He said.

Reggie put on his swim trunks and jumped in with Yolanda. Reggie was very handsome and looked like a model. He was six-foot-one, had an athletic build, caramel skin, a low-cut beard, and he looked handsome in a suit. He had a deep voice that made me weak and was comforting, and he had long eyelashes. The ladies loved Reggie, but they didn't want to deal with me. I grabbed a drink and sat on the lanai, watching them play in the pool. I imagined them being me and my dad. I thought more about him and planned to ask Momma when she arrives.

Momma is *very* rich. She inherited my grandparents' department store called *Robertson's*. Over the years, it grew nationwide. She later started her investment firm, and she was always on the go – networking and meetings. She lives in Texas but often flew here to visit. She's down to earth and never forgot where she came from. She was humble and would take the shirt off her back to help anyone in need. Everyone loved her and she was highly respected in the corporate world. She taught me everything I know; finances, real estate, and investing. Momma was smart and loved Reggie like a son. She spoiled Yolanda rotten, but Yolanda was a grateful girl, and Reggie and I are both big disciplinarians. Yolanda did her chores, made good grades, and wanted to follow our footsteps. Maybe she will take over the business when Reggie and I retire.

Dina

Chapter 4

I arrived at my office after being in court all morning, and I've been working on one case after another. I attended college here in New York and went to law school. I passed the bar the first time and started as a pro bono attorney. I was winning cases and after I made a name for myself, I worked for one of the top firms in the state, and later opened my own practice. I've had my practice for three years and it was just me and my legal assistant. I was always the bookworm of my sisters and work was my life. I'm single, never had children, and never been married. My high school sweetheart and I broke up after we graduated high school. I attended college in New York, and he attended college back home. I miss him at times and wonder how he was doing. I was crushed when we broke up. The long distant relationship wouldn't work for me, and I was determined to be successful. I got engaged while in law school but, things didn't work out. I haven't seen or heard from him since and it's been five years. I haven't been with a man or on a date since then, wrapped up in my work. I wasn't big on partying but the few times I did, I was the life of the party, next to Jaz. I was rarely seen but when I showed up, I automatically stole the spotlight, my sisters didn't mind. One thing about us was that we were never in competition with each other, and Daddy treated us equally. Alexis had a style everyone loved. Her hair was always done, she had the best wardrobe, and was trendy. Jaz was gorgeous; red bone, wore her hair natural, normally a big afro, or braids. She was thick and curvy and was the shortest of us. She was only five-foot-seven.

Alexis had a strong marriage and she and Patrick were the couple people admired. They were well established, and Alexis also gave good advice. I was secretly rooting for Kel and Jaz but, she had to move on with her life. Jaz and Kel were the popular couple back in the day. They were crazy about each other, but their relationship became rocky when she went to North Carolina for college. She told me about Carlin, and I was happy for her. Carlin was successful but had a dry sense of humor. He wasn't the type of guy Jaz would date – the corporate guy. Kel was her type. I often wondered if she was still in love with him. I think Carlin is jealous of Kel and married Jaz to keep her from going back to Kel. I never shared this with her or Alexis but, that was my theory. To my understanding, Carlin barely spent time with Jaz, and she was always alone. Carlin's work came first. He was nice but, that was it. There was no engaging with the family or anything. I'm anxious to see how long their marriage will last, and I think Jaz's emotions were getting the best of her.

My visit with Daddy was good. He looked weak and ready to give out. Although I live in New York, I'm still a *daddy's girl*. I call him almost every day and visit as much as I can. Alexis has been doing good taking care of him. Jaz looked as if something was on her mind. I know she's homesick but, something else is up. I don't think she's happy with Carlin like she pretends to be.

It was lunch time, and I grabbed my purse and walked out my office to my legal assistant. "Hey Keisha, I'm going to lunch, want anything?"

"Where are you going?" She asked.

"I'm just going to grab something to-go from the deli down the street."

"I'll take a chef salad."

"Alright, I'll be back."

Keisha was in her mid-twenties and a very smart girl. She was petite and maintained a healthy diet. I, on the other hand, ate junk food, and then burned it off. It was cold outside and a crowd of people walking the streets of Manhattan. I picked up our lunch and hurried back to the office. Keisha and I ate lunch in the conference room and returned to our desks afterwards. "Oh Dina, an Andrew Hicks called while you were out." She said. "He insisted on speaking with you directly and left his phone number."

"Thanks." I dialed his number.

"Hello?" A man answered.

"Hello, this is La'Dina James. I was returning Andrew Hicks' call."

"This is Andrew. I want to schedule a consultation with you. My wife and I are getting a divorce."

"Okay, I'm free this afternoon if you would like to come in."

"That will be great. I can be there in an hour if that's okay?"

"Great. The first consultation is three-hundred dollars."

"Okay, see you then."

I had Keisha put him on my calendar and prepared for the consultation. Soon, she paged me. "Miss. James, Andrew Hicks is here to see you." She said. "He's finishing up the form."

"Okay, thank you."

Keisha brought me his profile and I checked it out. He was referred to me by a former client of mine. He's an ER surgeon, and his wife is unemployed. This is a fight, already. I then walked out to the lobby. "Mr. Hicks?" He stood and he was *fine*. He was very tall and wore a nice suit. I walked up to him and extended my hand. "I'm La'Dina James, it's nice to meet you."

"Likewise." He said, smiling.

"Follow me." We walked in my office, and he sat across from my desk. "Okay, let's get started."

Andrew explained everything to me. He caught his wife in bed with another man in their condo. They have a house, three vehicles, and she wants half of his dad's inheritance. While we were talking, I found myself looking at his dark, smooth skin and big eyes. "Mia is threatening to take everything I have." He said. "I don't want that to happen."

"I understand. I will do the best I can, and I will be in touch. If you have any questions, contact me, or leave a message with my assistant, Keisha."

"Okay, thank you, Mrs. James." He said.

"Oh, it's *Miss.* James."

"I'm sorry."

"That's okay." We shook hands and he left.

I started on Andrew's case and worked on other cases. Later, Keisha and I closed the office and walked outside. "I'll see you on Monday."

"Have a good weekend." Keisha said, walking to her car.

I walked in my condo and kicked off my heels. I turned on the heater and took a shower. I then put on my warm lounging clothes and ordered a pizza. I poured myself a glass of wine and looked at my view of the Manhattan Bridge. I sat there, looking at the city lights and remembered that my lease was expiring soon. I was indecisive about buying a house or renewing my lease. I then thought about Jaz and Daddy and decided to call Daddy first. "Hello?" He answered.

"Hi Daddy, how are you?"

"Hey Dina. I'm doing good. How about you?"

"I'm fine. I'm thinking about buying a house."

"Oh, you're finally buying one?" He asked.

"I'm thinking about it. How have you been feeling?"

"I've been feeling good. I have my good days and my bad days. Alexis makes sure I take my medicine."

"How is Alexis?"

"She's fine. Call her."

"I'll call her tomorrow. I've been thinking about Jaz a lot since I left there."

"So have I." He said. "I talked to her yesterday, and she seemed alright. She's always hiding her emotions, but I can read right through her."

Daddy was right and he would catch us in a lie before we could think of one. "She doesn't seem happy. I can tell she's homesick too."

"She is, and I believe she's happy with Carlin. But I think she still has feelings for Kel too."

"I agree. I'm keeping my thoughts to myself around her. But I know her heart is with Kel."

"She has to work through this on her own." He said. "Are you still coming for Thanksgiving?"

"I will be there. Well Daddy, I'm going to call Jaz. I'll talk to you later."

"Alright, baby girl. Let me know how the house hunting goes."

"I will. I love you."

"I love you too." He said. We hung up and I called Jaz.

She was fussing at MJ. "Hello?" She answered.

"Hey Jaz, it's Dina."

"What's up?"

"Why are you fussing at my nephew?"

"Girl, he has this thing about stuffing his mouth. Then he started choking."

"Oh, he's just a kid."

"Anyway, what's going on with you?" She asked.

"Nothing, I just got off the phone with Daddy."

"How is he?"

"He sounded good. We didn't talk long. I was thinking about you and him."

"Oh, how nice." She said. "What are your plans for the weekend?"

"Well, my lease expires soon so I'm house hunting."

"Good luck."

"Jaz, is everything okay with you at home?"

She paused. "Yeah, why?"

"Because you acted as if something was wrong when you left Texas."

"Dina, I'm fine." She said. "You and Daddy worry too much over nothing. Alexis keeps her mouth closed."

That's because she knows its Carlin. "Okay, I'll call you tomorrow and update you on the house."

"Alright, sis, love you!"

"Love you too."

We hung up and I started wondering what Alexis would say about Jaz. But I know she's just going to say '*I'm staying out of it. She's just going to have to find out on her own. I told her not to marry him*'.

Alexis

Chapter 5

Tomorrow is Thanksgiving and we decided to have dinner at Dad's house this year. Dina will be in town this afternoon and Jaz and Carlin been here all week. MJ was with Kel. There was something about Carlin that I did not like. Jaz told me when they arrived that Kel was picking up MJ from my house because Carlin didn't want her going to his house. If it weren't for Jaz, Carlin wouldn't be staying in our house. He spent most of the time here on his laptop working. I'd rather Jaz and MJ come without him. It was obvious that Kel didn't like Carlin either. He respected Carlin as Jaz's husband but, Carlin doesn't want any problems out of Kel or his brother. Kel has a past and used to run with Traci's brother. They have a reputation. Kel would literally kill for his family, and Jaz. This week has been a challenge for me with Carlin being here, but he and Patrick were getting along. Dina was staying with Dad. Jaz wanted to but Carlin didn't. I think he envies her relationship with Dad. I can't stand him!

I had one of the other stylists straighten my hair for the holidays. I went to the grocery store, picked up two deep fried turkeys from Traci's restaurant, and dropped the food off at Dad's house. I'm looking forward to cooking tonight.

Later, Jaz and I went to Dad's house. We left the guys and my boys at home. Dad was getting dressed to go out, and soon Dina arrived. She looked pretty as always, and she got settled. We were talking in the den and soon, Dad walked out of his bedroom, dressed up. "Where are you going?" Dina asked him.

"I'm going out!" Dad said, grabbing his keys.

"Daddy, are you able to drive?" Jaz asked.

"Jaz, I'm not crippled. I can still drive. Go on and have fun. I'll be fine. Don't worry about me." He left.

"Is he going to be okay?" Jaz asked.

"Girl, yes. Trust me. He's probably hanging out with Uncle Ernest."

We started cooking the Thanksgiving dinner. I was making the dressing and peach cobbler. Jaz was making the broccoli and rice casserole and peeled the potatoes for the potato salad. Dina started picking greens and was making a pineapple upside down cake, and the ham. Dina turned Dad's stereo on and played old songs we grew up listening too. We were dancing, singing, and cooking. I haven't seen Jaz have this much fun in a long time. Dina was the bookworm but, she knew how to have fun also. I missed my sisters, and I was taking pictures of us, posting them on my social media pages. I always imagined me, Patrick, and our boys hanging out with my sisters and their families. Jaz would be with Kel and Dina would be married. Maybe this will happen one day.

While dancing, I thought about telling them about my interest in finding our mom and turned the music down. "Hey!" Jaz said.

"Why you turn the music down?" Dina asked.

"I have a question."

"What's wrong?" Jaz asked.

"I've been thinking about this for a while, and I never told Dad. Have you thought about finding our mother?"

Dina and Jaz looked at each other. "I haven't." Jaz said.

"I've wondered where she was but, I've never given it much thought." Dina said.

"I want to find her."

"You may have to start with Daddy." Dina said.

"I know but, I don't want him wondering around, trying to find her."

"Do you have a plan?" Jaz asked.

"No, I don't know where to start."

"Well, Daddy is your only option." Dina said. "But when will you have the time to do all of this? You have the boys, your hours at the salon can be crazy, and you're back and forth with Daddy."

I thought about it. My schedule can be crazy, along with Dad and my boys. "Y'all are right. Let's keep this between us but, I do plan to find her."

It's Thanksgiving Day and we're all at Dad's house, eating. We finished cooking at three o'clock this morning, laughing, dancing, and talking. Dad came home early and went straight to bed. "Christmas will be at our house this year." Jaz announced.

"Okay." Dad said. "I can get out of Texas for a change."

"I have an announcement too." Dina said. "I bought a brownstone in Brooklyn, and I move next week."

"I can't wait to see it."

"Congratulations." Dad said.

"We can celebrate the holidays at your house now." Jaz said.

Later, my sisters and I cleaned up, and the guys watched the game in the den. Afterwards, we sat at the dining room table and talked. I told them about Dad's doctor's appointment for Tuesday, and we planned the Christmas dinner. Thanksgiving dinner was a good turnout, although I didn't care for Carlin's presence. He was a good-looking guy and very successful but, I didn't like how he treated my sister or his jealousy of her connection to Kel. There was no doubt that Jaz still had feelings for Kel, and Carlin probably sensed it.

We're back at home, and we put our leftovers in the kitchen. Jaz and Carlin went to bed, and the boys went to their bedrooms. Patrick and I changed and lied in the bed. "Are you okay, baby?" He asked.

"I'm alright. Last night, I shared with Jaz and Dina about me wanting to find our mother."

"What did they say?"

"They didn't seem bothered at all and Dina doesn't think I will have the time to find her."

"Well, let me know and I'll help you. This is obviously something that you're determined to do, and you have the right to know who she is."

"I'm still going to look for her. What are your thoughts on Carlin?"

"Baby, you know I'm neutral but, he is definitely jealous of Kel." He said.

If Patrick noticed something, it was true. He never complained about anything and didn't have an enemy. "I think Jaz is lonely and he puts his work before her."

"Kel is cool, and he and I always got along. But that's them. Just be there for your sister when needed. I don't want you caught up in whatever Carlin has going on. I know you don't care for him but stay away."

"I know and I was nice the entire time."

"I know and I'm glad you were." He said. "But stand clear because if he comes for you, I'm definitely go after him."

Jaz

Chapter 6

It's Christmas Eve, and Daddy, my sisters, and nephews arrived yesterday. I was excited to see them, and their loving energy filled the house. We're all drinking coffee and my nephews were upstairs playing with MJ. Later, we went to the grocery store and the guys stayed at the house. We went back to the house and started picking greens and peeling potatoes. Carlin lit the fireplace and it set the holiday mood. Our house was professionally decorated, and we had a huge Christmas tree in the family room. Alexis played her Christmas playlist while we were cooking. I grabbed a bottle of red wine out of the wine cellar and poured us each a glass.

The doorbell rang, and Carlin answered it. "Hello." Denise said, walking in the kitchen.

"Hey Denise. Girls, this is my college friend, Denise. Denise, this is my big sister, Alexis."

Alexis extended her arm and Denise barely shook it. "Nice to meet you." She said.

Alexis looked at her like she was crazy. "Uh, and this is my little sister Dina."

Dina shook her hand. "Nice to meet you."

"Likewise." Denise said. "Where did Carlin go?"

"He's with my dad and Alexis' husband in the billiard room." Denise walked off.

"I know you saw how she looked at me." Alexis said.

"Oh, that's just how she is. She means no harm."

"Jaz, I noticed how she looked at us too." Dina said. "She acted like she didn't want to shake my hand either."

"Look, can we just cook and not worry about her. Denise and I went to college together and we're good friends."

Alexis walked out the kitchen and returned. "Hmm, she looks a little too friendly with Carlin to me." Alexis said.

"She's just a friendly person."

"Jaz, are you that naïve?" Dina asked, looking at me. "She's a *jealous* person."

"Have you ever mentioned us to her?" Alexis asked.

"I told her that I have two sisters. Now, can we get back to cooking?"

Denise walked back in the kitchen. "Well Jaz, I'm going to see my parents." She said. "We have family from out of town too."

Alexis sized her up and Dina rolled her eyes. "Okay Denise. Have a Merry Christmas."

"You too." She left.

"Do y'all have to be so rude?"

Dina laughed. "Does *she* have to be so rude?" Alexis asked.

"I don't like her." Dina said.

"Neither do I and I don't trust her." Alexis said.

"Okay, let's get back to cooking."

It's Christmas morning and we're all sitting around the tree, opening gifts. Alexis and Patrick brought their sons' gifts here to open with MJ. Kel sent MJ money and a few presents. Carlin didn't seem pleased but when it came to my son's relationship with is dad, his opinion didn't matter.

After we opened gifts, we got dressed for dinner. We didn't finish cooking until two o'clock this morning. After we got dressed, I let MJ talk to his dad and Carlin didn't look happy. Alexis was mean mugging him, waiting for him to say something. We set the table in the formal dining room and Carlin lit the fireplace. Dina and Alexis warmed up the food and I put them in our serving entrees. We sat around the table and Daddy said the prayer. We began eating and Alexis played her Christmas playlist again.

The food was good, and I was stuffed. We were laughing and talking, and some were eating dessert. "Ladies, you cooked a good dinner." Daddy complimented.

"Thank you."

"Everything was good."

"The peach cobbler was a hit, baby." Patrick said to Alexis.

"Thank you."

Patrick and Alexis have been married for fifteen years and still acted like newlyweds. Unfortunately, Carlin and I weren't like that. Dina is single with no life but, she knew how to have fun. Daddy has dated on and off over the years but never married. I often wondered if he got lonely. Maybe Daddy should start dating. The boys went upstairs, and we continued talking. "Daddy, have you ever thought about dating?"

He looked at me like I was crazy. "Jaz, I have enough going on than to worry about dating." He said. "I'm in my sixties and I've had my share of women."

"Can you give us advice on life?" Dina asked.

"Well, life is short. Have fun, take care of yourselves, and be happy. It's that simple. I've been sick for years simply because I didn't take care of myself – eating bad, drinking, and smoking. It caught up with me. But I never let that stop me from having fun. I still hang out with the guys but sitting at home gives me peace of mind. I'm happy just doing that. Never let anyone or anything get to you. If you find yourself getting angry or if you're unhappy about something, address it. If it goes well, come to an understanding, don't bring it up again, and move on. If it goes bad, walk away."

"Can you tell us about relationships?"

Daddy chuckled. "I've never been married." He said. "I just had beautiful girls. Y'all became my priority, and I enjoyed raising all of you. Being a dad to girls wasn't easy but I did it."

"Well Dad, you did an amazing job raising us." Alexis said, smiling. "Dad, I have a question for you, and it's been on my mind for a while. Where is our mother?"

Daddy paused. "I don't know." He said. "All I know is that she lives in Fort Worth. I wish I could tell you more but, I haven't talked to her in over ten years. MJ was a newborn, and your boys were little. Alexis, if you want to find her, go for it. You have every right to know who she is but, all I can tell you is Fort Worth."

Its eight o'clock in the evening and we're all in the family room, quiet. I was thinking about Alexis wanting to find our mother. Her question was the elephant in the room. The boys were still upstairs playing, and we had the fireplace going. The TV was off, and the only sound was the crackling from the fire. Alexis and Patrick were hugged up together and Dina was sitting next to Daddy, staring into space. Carlin was sitting in the recliner with his eyes closed, and I sat alone. "So, what's everyone's plans for New Years?" Daddy asked, breaking the silence.

"We don't have any plans." Alexis said.

"Carlin and I are going to a party."

"I'm going to Times Square." Dina said.

"I'm staying in the house." Daddy said, sipping his brandy.

Daddy pulled out his cigar and walked out to the covered patio. Patrick kissed Alexis and the guys joined him. "Alexis, are you serious about finding our mother?" Dina asked.

"Yes, I'm going to find our mother." Alexis said. "Dad did a wonderful job raising us but, he never mentioned her to us and that bothers me. Why hasn't he talked about her? Why didn't they get married since they had three girls? Something must have happened and he's not saying much about it."

"Why didn't you ask him?"

"Jaz, you know how Dad is." Alexis said. "He shuts down and I don't want him to get upset. Dad is finally getting better, and I don't want him worrying about me finding our mom. But I am curious about how y'all feel?"

"I'm okay with it."

We turned to Dina. "I'm fine too." She said. "Let me know if you need help."

Yvette

Chapter 7

Reggie and I are hosting a New Year's party at our house. We had a full house, and we were all dancing to old-school hip-hop music. Yolanda was upstairs playing with other kids and Momma was here, dancing like a teenager. We had a deejay, plenty of food, and cases of Dom Perignon. Reggie and I were dancing, all over each other, and we also had a crowd outside on the lanai. Some people were in the pool and upstairs on the loft and deck.

We spent Thanksgiving in Texas with Momma and spent Christmas here at home. I still haven't asked Momma about my dad but planned too. That was one goal for the new year, to find my dad. I walked around looking for Reggie.

The countdown was getting closer, and I finally found him at the barbeque pit. "Hey Reggie, it's almost time for the countdown."

"Alright, let's pass out the bottles of champagne." He said.

We handed out the bottles and Momma called for the kids to come downstairs. We all stood around and the music was turned down. This year was a success. Our business was still growing, and we were looking to expand. We did the countdown and popped champagne bottles. Reggie and I kissed, and hugged Yolanda. "I love you, Reggie."

He kissed me. "I love you too, baby." The kids went back upstairs, and the party continued.

Momma and Reggie's mother cooked a big New Year's dinner. We ate our black-eyed peas and there was a lot of leftover food from last night. The party didn't end until four o'clock this morning and I'm sore from dancing. Our families left and Momma was flying to Florida on business this evening. Reggie was taking a nap, and Yolanda was in her bedroom watching TV.

"Thanks for the dinner. It was good."

"You're welcome, sweetie." Momma said, putting plates in a bag. "I'm glad you liked it. Thanks for having me over. I was going to sit at home and do nothing."

"No problem. Can I ask you a question?"

"Sure!"

"Where is my dad?"

Momma paused and slowly put her bag down. She turned around with a blank look on her face. "I don't know. I haven't heard from him in over ten years, and he was living in Fort Worth, Texas at the time. I don't know if he's still living there or not."

"I want to meet him. If you talk to him again, find out where he is, please?"

"I promise." She said.

Later, Momma had a car pick her up. I hope she finds my dad. Reggie was still asleep, and Yolanda eventually fell asleep. I sat in the family room, thinking about my dad. I'm starting my year off with finding him and meeting his side of the family. I couldn't wait to tell Reggie when he wakes up. I relaxed and closed my eyes. I was tired and had a lot on my mind. One thing about being an entrepreneur was that my brain was always going. Not to mention me finding my family and wanting another baby.

Reggie woke up and he joined me. "I asked my mom about my dad."

Reggie turned to me. "What did she say?" He asked.

"She told me that she hasn't talked to him in ten years and he was living in Fort Worth, Texas at the time. She doesn't know if he's still living there or not."

"She'll find him, baby."

"I always wondered if I had brothers or sisters, or if I was an only child."

"Well, start searching."

"Fort Worth is all I have and if I do have brothers or sisters, why hasn't my mom told me about them?"

"Don't jump to conclusions, Yvette." He said. "Just start with Fort Worth and when you get results, question her then."

Reggie was always supportive and gave the best advice. "Reggie, I want another baby."

"Whoa! You're full of surprises, aren't you?"

"I'm sorry. My plans this year is to find my family and get pregnant again."

Reggie raised his eyebrows and looked at me, smiling. I knew what that meant. "Well, you know we can always practice." He said.

"Let me check on Yolanda." I ran upstairs and Reggie ran to our bedroom. I opened her bedroom door, and she was in her pajamas, watching TV. "Goodnight, Yolanda."

"Goodnight, Momma." She said. "Can I watch TV in bed?"

"You can until this show goes off."

"Okay." I turned out her light and closed her door.

I ran downstairs and turned off everything. I went into our bedroom and Reggie was laying in the bed, under the sheets, modeling. I laughed at how silly he was acting, and the practice began.

Dina

Chapter 8

I'm all moved in my new brownstone. It was a three-story with four bedrooms, a two-car garage, and a basement. It was spacious. There was a fireplace in the kitchen, the living room, and the master bedroom. I also had an office. I loved my new place and couldn't wait to finish unpacking. I haven't talked to my sisters since Christmas, but we wished each other a *Happy New Year* through text messages. Alexis was planning to search for our mother and Jaz was still doing her thing, whatever that was. I was busy with work, moving, and thought about Daddy.

I arrived at the office and went inside. "Good morning, Keisha."

"Hey Dina, how was your New Years?" She asked, brewing coffee.

"It was good." She followed me to my office. "What did you do?"

"I went to a party in Brooklyn. It was nice, what about you?"

"I went to Time Square, for the first time with a few friends from college."

"I never been, as long as I lived here." She said. "What was it like?"

"It was very crowded. I saw celebrities, people running naked through the crowd, and a lot of drunk people. But the countdown was the best part."

"We didn't watch it on TV. It was an ongoing party."

We went back to work and later, Keisha informed me that Andrew Hicks was back, and she sent him to my office. "How are you Mr. Hicks?"

"I'm fine, how are you?" He asked, walking in, dressed in scrubs.

"I'm good. Have a seat."

"Thanks, Happy New Year."

"Happy New Year to you too. So, how can I help you?"

He sat back in the chair and sighed. "La'Dina...can I call you La'Dina?" He asked.

"You can call me Dina."

"Dina, I'm ready for this divorce to be final. She is getting on my last nerve."

"What's going on?"

"She wants the house, the condo, the cars, and half of my inheritance." He said.

"Where does she expect you to live?"

"She expects me to buy my own place."

No she didn't. "Okay, I've been out of town and your case is the newest one I have. I'm working on it and I'll let you know when your court date is. But hang in there and I promise you that I will do the best I can. You picked a good lawyer and I'm well known."

He laughed. "I hope you have connections because she's trying to break me."

"You'll be fine. I filed your petition, and we're waiting on your court date."

"What happens then?" He asked.

"We will meet with your wife and her attorney to see if we can come to a settlement."

"Okay, I came to pay you also. I gave it to Keisha." He stood and just as he was about to walk out of my office, he turned around and sat back down. "Dina, can I ask you a personal question?"

"What's that?"

"Do you have a man?"

I chuckled. "No, I don't."

"I don't want you to feel uncomfortable and I understand that you have to be professional but, I find you very attractive." He said.

My heart was skipping beats. He was *so* fine, and I always get butterflies when we talk. "Thanks."

"I would love to take you out sometime, if you'd like?"

Stay professional, Dina. "I'm sorry Mr. Hicks, but I don't mix business with pleasure. I'm going through enough now, and I just don't have the time."

He stood. "Well, it was worth a shot." He said. "I'll see you soon." He left.

I have no time for games. Besides, he's vulnerable and still married.

Later, I got my things together and left for the day. I stopped for a burger and went home. It was freezing outside, and my townhome was cold. I turned my heater on, took a shower, put on my sweats, and built a fire in my oversized fireplace. I ate and poured myself a glass of red wine. I looked around my townhome and planned to finish decorating. I sat by my fireplace, wrapped in a quilt that my grandmother made for me when I was little, listening to music. I started thinking about Alexis looking for our mother. I had mixed feelings about finding her and often thought about her, growing up. Ever since Alexis asked Daddy about our mother, it's been on my mind. I began to wonder where she was and why she abandoned us. My sisters and I are tall, and we obviously got our height from Daddy. He was six-foot-four, but I wonder if our mom was tall. I then began to wonder if we had other siblings, nieces, and nephews. I hope Alexis is successful and I offered my help if needed. I then thought about my personal life. I was single and didn't have a male friend. I guess Andrew could be my friend but, he is my client. I can't do that, and I don't want there to be any problems. He was very good looking, successful, had no children, and I was curious to learn more about him. There wouldn't be a reason for him and his wife to communicate after their divorce is final. I may reconsider if he asks me out again.

Alexis

Chapter 9

I've been calling Dad all day, and he hasn't answered. I was getting nervous. I finished with my client and called him again, there was no answer. I tried his cell phone, no answer. Something is wrong. I left work and went straight to his house. His truck was here, parked crooked. I went inside and didn't see him. I called for him and heard a slight moan coming from the bedroom. I ran to the back and Dad was sitting on the bed, leaning forward. I looked in his face and one side was slightly drooped. I immediately called 9-1-1 and followed them to the hospital. I called Patrick and then my sisters. They both were in a panic and insisted on flying down and were booking their flights. I called Uncle Ernest, but he was on the road. He's a truck driver. I told him I would keep him informed.

We arrived at the hospital and the paramedic wheeled Dad inside. I sat in the waiting area, nervous. I began to shake, and tears filled my eyes. What if we lose Dad? I waited for a long time and Patrick finally arrived. He saw how distraught I was and wrapped his arms around me, kissing my cheeks. "Any news?" He asked.

"No, not yet. Where are the boys?"

"They're at my brother's house. How are you holding up, baby?"

"Patrick, I'm scared." Tears ran down my face. "I can't lose him."

Patrick held me and we continued to wait. Dad's doctor, Roslyn finally walked out. "Mr. Morris is fine." She said.

"What happened?"

"He had a stroke." My heart skipped beats. "His blood pressure was 160/100. We're going to keep him overnight to monitor him and run more tests."

"Can I see him?"

"It will be while." She said. "But the visit will have to be brief. He is awake and alert, and his memory seems fine. I will let you know when you can see him."

"Thank you, Roslyn." She walked off.

I was relieved and Patrick held me. "At least he's fine, baby." He said.

"Patrick, what if I didn't go over there? What if I didn't call to check on him?"

"Baby, stop thinking like that." He said. "I know you're scared but, he is fine. Thank God you thought to check on him and got there in time. Where are your sisters?"

"Jaz is landing soon, and Dina is still on the plane."

"Okay, are you hungry?"

"I don't have an appetite."

"You need to eat, Alexis."

"I know but, I have to see and talk to my dad first."

"Okay afterwards, I'm taking you to get something to eat, baby." He said.

We waited and soon, Jaz arrived. We hugged and I told her what happened. "Thank God you got there on time." She said.

"Roslyn said we can see him. He's alert and his memory is fine. Where is my nephew?"

"I dropped him off with Kel."

"Your husband didn't come?"

"No, he's working." *That figures.* "Any word from Dina?"

"Her plane lands in another hour."

Roslyn came out and we stood. "Okay, we gave him some medication for his blood pressure." She said. "He is awake and alert but, he can't have any excitement."

"Thank you, Roslyn." She told us where Dad was, and we went to see him.

We walked in the room and Dad was lying down, half asleep. He slowly turned his head to see us and gave a slight smile. "Hey." He said.

"Hi Daddy." Jaz said, hugging him. "You scared us."

"Oh, I'm fine." He said. "You didn't have to fly all the way here."

"Yes, I did." She said. "Dina is on a plane now. She should be landing shortly."

Dad then turned to me and Patrick and spoke. "How are you feeling?"

"I'm alright." He said. "I'm just a little high."

We visited with Dad, and Patrick left to pick up the boys. Soon, Dina called letting us know she was on her way from the airport. Jaz and I decided to wait for her. Dad was still awake but looked sleepy. He dozed off and I chatted with Jaz. I could tell she was homesick. She looked as if something was on her mind. "Are you okay, Jaz?"

"I'm fine." She said, looking confused.

"How is everything at home?"

"It's okay. I've been busy with the vineyard and the stores, and Carlin is busy with the dealerships."

She's lying. Dina walked in and we hugged her. She hugged Dad and visited with him. I was hungry and emotionally exhausted. I hugged and kissed Dad and left. Jaz and Dina stayed. I called Patrick when I got in the car. "Hey, baby." He answered. "Is everything okay?"

"Yes, I'm on my way home. Jaz and Dina are still with Dad. They're going to stay at his house."

"I bought food. There is plenty if your sisters want to come."

He was so thoughtful. "Thank you, baby."

I walked in the house and Patrick and the boys hugged me. I ate and hung out with them. We explained to the boys what was going on with their grandfather. They were teens and had a lot of questions. They loved their grandfather and had been spending time with him. Jaz and Dina came over and ate and went to Dad's house.

I relaxed in the family room. Patrick cleaned the kitchen and sat next to me. "You alright?" He asked.

"I will be. Oh, Patrick, I'm a nervous wreck and Dad acts like nothing is wrong."

I tried to hold back my tears, but they began to flow.

"He'll be fine, baby." He wrapped his arms around me. "Just be strong and remember that I'm here for you."

"Yeah. I'm going to bed." He followed me in the bedroom. "How are the boys?"

"They're fine." He said. "They understand. But I think they're worried about you."

"I'm sure they are. I'll take them to school in the morning and talk to them again."

It's Friday morning and I just dropped the boys off at school. I was going to the salon after I visit Dad. I went to the hospital and Dina and Jaz were here. Dad was watching TV, talking to us. He seemed better but they were keeping him. "I have some news for y'all." Dad said. We gave him our undivided attention. "I talked to your momma the other day. She was in Florida on business. She had my number all this time but never called."

"Where is she?"

"She lives in Fort Worth in a wealthy community called Winter Hills."

Our mouths dropped. "Those are all mansions."

"What does she do?" Dina asked.

"She owns Robertson's department store." Dad said. "It has been a family-owned business for years. She also owns an investment firm downtown called *Robertson's Inc*. Your momma and I never got married, we just had beautiful girls together. She was always gone on business, and I took care of Alexis and Jaz while she was gone. We broke up and I kept y'all. I dated another woman named Sylvia but, I loved your momma so much that I went back to her about two years later. Then she got pregnant with Dina."

"Really?" Jaz asked. "So, y'all split up after Dina was born?"

"Yes. I kept Dina and she went on about her business. She would call and check on y'all but, that was it."

"So, her business was more important than us?"

"Alexis, don't say that." Dad said. "I told her that if she wasn't going to be in your lives, I was going to get custody. I did and she got visitation rights but, she never visited. I raised y'all on my own."

"Does she know that you're sick?"

"I've been a diabetic since Dina was born." Dad said. "She knew that but, I didn't tell her about me being in and out of the hospital. She lives in the bricked wall area of Winter Hills, but you can barely see her house. I didn't get her address, we didn't talk long. Alexis, if you still want to find her, that's a start. I don't know what's going to happen while I'm in the hospital but, I think God is trying to tell us something by your momma calling me out the blue."

We nodded. "So, how will I know its Mom if I see her?"

"Jaz looks identical to her." Dad said. "When you meet her, don't get mad or get an attitude with her, none of you. Get to know her and listen to her. She's a very strong and genuine woman. She's also smart and that's where Dina gets her business sense from. Jaz gets her shopping habits from her, and you get your patience from her. She and I are going to talk more about her reuniting with you all soon. But love your momma and give her another chance, I mean it." Dad demanded.

We looked at each other and nodded. After visiting with Dad, I left. My sisters stayed. I'm excited to find out who our mom is but at the same time, I'm confused and angry. But Dad made it plain and clear that he wanted us to respect her.

Jaz

Chapter 10

MJ and I are on our way home from the airport. Daddy wasn't getting any better or worse. Kel was excited to see MJ and he took our son to visit Daddy. Kel and Daddy had a good relationship. He treated both Patrick and Kel like the sons he never had. Dina flew back to New York this morning and Alexis was going to keep us updated. I told Carlin that we would be home tomorrow, but I missed him and thought I'd surprise him a day early.

The Uber drove up to our house and the driver helped us with our luggage. I went inside and sent MJ up to his bedroom to unpack. I walked through the house, looking for Carlin but didn't see him. I went in the family room and saw strawberries and champagne on the coffee table. My heart started racing when I saw lipstick on one of the glasses. I then heard a funny noise coming from our bedroom. I slowly walked towards the bedroom and took off my heels to keep quiet. I walked into our master foyer and heard a screeching noise. I cracked the door open and froze. Carlin and Denise were having sex in our bed. I charged at her and hit her in the back of her head. Carlin jumped up and ran in the bathroom while I was fighting Denise. Carlin then pulled me off her after seeing blood. "Get off of me!"

"Jaz, calm down!" He yelled.

"Calm down? I just saw y'all having sex in my bed!"

"Jaz, I can explain." Denise said, out of breath.

"No, I want both of y'all out of my house!"

"I'm not going anywhere!" He demanded.

"You better get the hell out of my house now!" I then turned to Denise. "You were supposed to be my friend! I'm out of town, worried about my sick father and you're sleeping with my husband!"

Denise didn't say anything and began to get dressed. "Jaz, I can explain." He said.

"Explain what? Get out!"

"Jaz, this is *his* house!" Denise yelled.

"You need to get out! You don't run shit around here!"

"Look Carlin, if you want me to leave, I'll leave." She said.

I turned to Carlin. "Stay. We can talk about this."

I calmly walked to the closet, pulled out my shotgun, loaded it, and cocked it. They were still in the bedroom, and I started shooting. Denise ran out and I was still shooting. Her SUV was parked on the side of the house. She burned off and I went back in after Carlin. "Get out! All this time you were gone on your so-called trips, you were with her! Carlin, my dad is still in the hospital." I began to cry. "I expected to come home to my husband for comfort and this is what I find!" He was silent. "Get out."

"Jaz, I'm not going anywhere." He said.

I aimed at him and started shooting again. He ducked and ran out the door and left.

I put the shotgun back and went upstairs to check on MJ. I took a deep breath before walking into his bedroom. He had his headphones on, playing his video game. "Are you okay?"

"Yes, what was that loud noise?" He asked.

"Oh, it was nothing. How would you like to go stay with Aunt Dina?"

"Can we?" He asked, getting excited.

"Of course. I want you to pack everything you have so we can stay at a hotel, okay?"

"Okay."

"I'll be back." I hurried downstairs.

I put my shotgun back in the case and put it in the back of my SUV. I went back inside and began packing MJ's clothes, and everything else that was his. I was full of adrenaline. I arranged for movers to pick up his bedroom furniture and deliver them to my storage this evening. I packed my belongings and MJ rode with me to open a storage unit across town, so Carlin won't do anything with our things. I paid with cash and loaded the storage unit with everything in my SUV, including my shotgun. I purchased boxes, and we went back to the house. Carlin was still gone, and I boxed up the rest of my things. The movers arrived and loaded up MJ's bedroom furniture and the rest of our things. I parked the SUV in the garage and switched to my Benz. The movers had all our things loaded in the truck and ready to be delivered to my storage. After everything was out, I did a final walk through in the house. MJ won't be back in this house anymore.

"Momma, why are we packing everything?" He asked.

"I'll tell you later, okay?"

"Okay." I took the spare key to my Benz and left.

The movers followed us to the storage and loaded our things in the unit. Afterwards, MJ and I checked-in at a hotel outside the city. I sat, trying to gather my thoughts. I had been moving non-stop all day and was trying to hold it together for my son. "MJ come here. I want to talk to you." He walked over to me. "We are moving in with Aunt Dina for a little while."

"Why, is Carlin coming too?" He asked.

"No, he's not. Carlin and I aren't going to be together anymore."

"Why?"

"We decided to break up. Carlin is too busy with work and other things."

"Okay." He said.

I then came up with a great idea for MJ. "How would you like to stay with your dad?"

"Can I?" He asked, getting excited.

"You sure can. He would love to keep you. Momma is going to stay with Aunt Dina and take care of a few things."

"Are you going to move back to Texas?"

"Yes, I am. That way you can be around me and Daddy all you want."

"Cool!"

He hugged me. "Are you hungry?"

"Yes."

"Okay, I'll order some food and we can eat and watch TV. But I want you to go to bed early because we're leaving early in the morning."

"Okay."

"Now, go wash up." He took off.

Later, I sent MJ to bed. He was excited about going to stay with his dad but, I was hurt about what happened. I couldn't believe what Carlin and my best friend did. I walked in the living area and cried. I was frustrated with everything that was going on.

I then called Dina. "Hello?" She answered.

"Hey Dina, it's Jaz."

"Hey Jaz! What's up?"

"MJ and I are coming to stay with you tomorrow."

"What happened?" I explained everything that happened and told her that I packed everything MJ and I owned and stored it. "I can't believe him!" She said. "Are you okay?"

"I'm fine. I'm staying in a hotel now."

"Okay, there is plenty of room here." She said. "Let me know when you arrive."

We hung up and I called Alexis explaining everything to her. "I told you Denise was up to no good." She said.

"I know. We're driving to New York in the morning to stay with Dina. I'm going to call Kel when I get there and talk to him about MJ moving with him."

"Good."

"I'm going to stay with Daddy when I get there. But don't tell him what's going on. I'll talk to him."

"No problem."

"How is Daddy, anyway?"

"Still the same." She said. "His blood pressure is slowly getting back to normal. He'll be going home soon."

"Okay, I'll call you when we get to New York and let you know when we're flying down." We hung up and I stretched out in the bed.

I then thought about Kel. I don't know what to tell him but MJ moving in wouldn't be a problem. I plan to stay with Dina during the divorce process and later move in with Daddy until I find a house. I'm going to keep my divorce quiet around Daddy. I don't want him to get upset, although I could use his advice. I cried myself to sleep.

Yvette

Chapter 11

I wonder if Momma has heard anything from Daddy. I've been thinking about that since I talked to her about finding him. I turned around in my chair and looked out my office window. It was cloudy and humid. I looked over the city of L.A. and thought about opening more locations. That would make traveling easier and we're growing.

I went back to work, and my phone rang. "This is Yvette Mitchell."

"Hey, it's Momma."

"Hi Momma."

"How is business?" She asked.

"Business is going good."

"I was calling to talk to you about your dad."

My heart started racing. "I'm listening."

"I talked to him while I was in Florida. He lives in Fort Worth and turns out that he had the same phone number. Your dad retired from the post office. He's a diabetic and has been real sick lately but, that's all I can tell you. We didn't talk long because I had a meeting. But that's a start."

"Good, I want to meet him. Do you have his address?"

"No, I've never been there, he moved. I didn't tell him about you. I want to talk to him in person. I've been trying to call him all week, but I haven't gotten an answer. I will keep trying."

"Thanks! This made my day. I was just thinking about this too."

"No problem." She said. "I was also calling to tell you that I'm having a formal dinner party next weekend. You all should come."

"Oh, what's the occasion?"

"It's actually a business dinner but, you and Reggie can meet other investors and network."

"Okay, we'll be there."

"Also, I'm looking to buy another house." She said. "I travel to California a lot and thought I'd buy a house there."

"No problem. Do you know where?"

"I was thinking Newport Beach."

"You don't want to look at some in Malibu near us?"

She laughed. "No honey, I would still have to travel."

"Okay, I'll look at some houses and email them to you. Let me know what you think, and we can take a trip to look at them."

After work, I went home and told Reggie about our conversation about Daddy. "Well, just be patient and see what else your mom finds out." He said. "At least you know where he lives."

"I wish I knew his address. Momma said she's never been there. Also, we've been invited to my mom's business dinner next weekend."

"Okay. How was work?"

"It was okay, kind of slow and the rain made it worse. You know, while I was sitting there, I started thinking about opening more branches."

"We do need to open more, baby." He said. "Where else could we open one?"

"Let's start with Colorado, and then Texas."

"Why?"

"We've gained a lot of clients there and it will lighten our travel expenses. We are growing."

"You really think we'll have time to open other offices right now?"

"Of course."

"Okay, I'll start looking into it next week." He said. "I'm going to look into Las Vegas also."

I kissed him. "Let's go to the movies, or something."

"Okay, get dressed."

This was music to my ears. I was excited that Momma found Daddy. I hope she hears from him soon too. I wondered if I had any brothers or sisters. If so, Momma didn't mention them. So far, my year was going well. Momma found Daddy, Reggie and I have been trying to make another baby, and he agreed to open more office locations.

It's Saturday, and Reggie was gone. Yolanda and I went to my neighbor Lisa's house. She and I chatted on her patio and our daughters were inside playing.

Lisa and I caught up and I told her about me trying to find my dad. I needed her advice. "What if you have other brothers and sisters?" She asked.

"I would definitely question my mom. I would be upset but, I'd be excited to meet them."

"I'm happy for you, Yvette. I hope you find him. Are you and Reggie still working on baby number two?"

"Yes, and we're planning to open more office locations."

"That would be cool." She said. Lisa was always supportive. "You two have a lot going on but, it's exciting."

"So far, everything is going well."

Dina

Chapter 12

Jaz and I are at my house, discussing her divorce. I already knew she wanted me to represent her the minute she told me about Carlin and Denise. Jaz talked to Kel the day after she and MJ arrived, and he was excited about their son going living with him. Jaz was flying MJ to Texas in the morning to help him get settled. I could not believe what she told me about Carlin and Denise. My sister deserves better. I grabbed my legal notepad, and we sat in the living room while MJ was upstairs playing. She's not going to like the information I'm about to give her. "I have good news and bad news."

She sighed, sipping her wine. "What's the bad news?" She asked.

"You're not going to like this but the sooner we start, the better."

"Okay, what is it?"

"I know you want to be divorced as soon as possible, but, in the state of North Carolina, you and Carlin have to be separated for at least a year to be eligible for a divorce."

Jaz had a look of disappointment, and her eyes filled with tears. "Dina, I don't want him!" She cried.

"I know you don't. Filing a separation agreement isn't required but my legal advice is that you should, to avoid any legal issues."

Jaz wiped the tears from her eyes. "Dina, I'm planning to move to Texas. Can I live there during the legal separation?"

"Yes."

"What about alimony?" She asked. "Can I still get that? I don't trust Carlin with the vineyard either."

"You can ask for that but it's up to the judge to grant it."

Jaz slowly nodded her head. "Okay, I'll do that." She softly said. "What was the good news?"

"My Pro Hac Vice was granted. I'm your attorney."

She smiled. "Cool!"

"Okay, how many businesses do you have?"

"Two in different locations." She said.

"What are they?"

"We have the vineyard in Charlotte and four stores throughout North Carolina and surrounding states. The dealership is divided into four branches throughout the state also."

"Are there any investments?"

"We have seven million dollars in stocks and bonds."

"What about MJ?"

"Carlin has nothing to do with him." She said.

"Do y'all have any other houses?"

"No."

"What are you asking for in this separation?"

"I don't care about the dealerships. But I do want the vineyard and stores. I manage those."

"Do y'all have any other assets or liabilities?"

"Just the businesses, the house, and cars." She said.

"How many cars?"

"We have eight. I just want two, the Benz and the Escalade. He can have the other cars."

"What about the dealership?"

"I don't want anything to do with them."

"Are you sure?"

"Yes." She said. "I want this done as quick as possible."

"Okay, I'll prepare the statement tomorrow while you're gone and file it immediately."

"What if he refuses?"

"We can't force him to sign the legal separation agreement, but you can do mediation. You two will have to come to an agreement and both of you will have to sign it."

"I'll do that. I don't trust him."

"Okay, I need all financial statements and tax documents. I need all documents on your vineyard, liabilities, and assets. If Carlin does not agree to the legal separation, you can still move to Texas. You will need to change your address on your driver's license, register your vehicles there, and keep all financial accounts separate moving forward. But you're risking him taking over the vineyard during the separation. I need you to be prepared for that."

"I don't want that." She said.

"I know but, I need you to remain calm. If Carlin ends up running the vineyard during the separation, you will have a better chance on getting temporary alimony. Use that to take care of yourself and get settled in Texas. Consider it a break from work and traveling. You need one." She nodded.

"Okay, we're done for now. Do you have everything you want out the house?"

"Yes." She said. "The day I left, I opened a storage across town where he wouldn't think to go and stored all my things there."

Jaz and MJ were fast asleep. I was lying in bed thinking about everything. I was glad that she got away from Carlin, and her shooting at him and Denise was no surprise. Jaz was a sweetheart but was the total opposite when mad. She had Daddy's temper. I wonder if she and Kel would end up back together again. I think she should stay single to heal. I then thought about Andrew. He was good looking, and I admit that I do have a crush on him. But I wanted to keep things professional with him and see what happens later.

Jaz and MJ left this morning for Texas. I finished drafting her legal separation statement. I felt bad for Jaz and I'm going to do my best to get her what she deserves. Soon, Keisha paged me. "Miss. James, Mr. Hicks is here to see you." She said.

"Send him in." He walked in my office, looking good as usual. "Hello Mr. Hicks."

"Hello, Miss. Dina." He said. "Please, call me Andrew."

"Okay, Andrew, have a seat. What can I do for you?"

"Can we push this divorce?"

"Why?"

"Mia is driving me crazy. She's been acting crazy since she was served and now, she's threatening to take my Hummer. That's not going to happen. That's my pride and joy. Now, she's refusing the divorce."

"Mr. Hicks, do you want the divorce?"

"Yes!" He assured.

"I'll see to it."

"Okay." He said. "She's the one who can't handle it. She even called my mom back home, crying. My mom told me that she won't leave her alone and cussed her out. She didn't like her anyway."

I wanted to laugh. Mia seemed childish and I haven't met her yet. "Well, stay calm. I want you to document everything she's doing. Do not let tell her anything, don't make yourself noticeable."

"Alright. Also, she has a very bad attitude, and she thinks she's above everyone. She's also made it plain and clear that her aunt will be representing her, if I go forward with the divorce."

"Okay, that's fine."

"Dina, her aunt is a man eater and she's tough. I don't know what our chances would be."

"Andrew, please relax."

"Why do you seem so calm?" He asked.

"Andrew, I've worked many cases, worse than this one. I'm prepared."

"Her Aunt Joan is crazy."

"Her Aunt Joan?"

The name *Joan* did ring a bell. "Yes, Joan Allen." He said.

"I'll surprise you."

"Dina, will you have dinner with me?" He asked, randomly.

"Andrew, I'm your attorney and we have a case to concentrate on. I don't mix business with pleasure. So, can we keep this on a professional level?"

He raised his hands. "No problem. I'm sorry." He stood. "Thank you."

"Have a nice day." He left.

I hope I wasn't too harsh but, I have no time for dates or games. I'm in my thirties and every man I've met and dated still had some growing up to do. He's still married anyway, and I want to know what I would be getting myself into. I'll wait.

After Andrew walked out, Keisha walked in. "Is everything okay?" She asked.

"Yeah, he's just frustrated with the divorce."

"Oh. He seemed upset when he walked out."

"Guess who his wife's attorney will be."

"Who?"

"Joan Allen."

Keisha raised her eyebrows. "Joan Allen, the lady with the bad attitude?" She asked.

"Yes."

"She's known for breaking a man's pockets when it came to divorces."

"I know."

"This should be easy for you. You tore her up in court before."

"Yes but, Andrew doesn't know that. He's nervous and I have a surprise for him. Joan and I never got along."

"That's because you made her look bad, and your attitude is worse than hers." I looked at her like she was crazy. "I meant that in a good way."

"Okay Keisha. Andrew does not need to know that I've battled Joan Allen. I'll tell him later."

"Okay." She said. "You think Andrew will tell his wife who you are?"

"No, he's trying to avoid her."

"Dang, I wish I could watch you beat eat her in the case." She said.

"Well, I may need you for the second round. You can rest assure that this won't be easy. They have too much going on."

"Cool. Well, I'm about to lock up for the day."

"Me too."

After work, I went home and changed clothes. I looked in my refrigerator and saw that I had nothing to cook. I took a shower and put on my jeans, a long sleeve t-shirt, and sneakers. I put my long hair back in a ponytail and went to a seafood restaurant. I was seated at a table near the bar and ordered a glass of white wine. There was a small crowd, and the atmosphere was nice. I looked towards the door and couldn't believe who I saw walking my way. "Is anyone sitting here?" Andrew asked.

I smiled. "No, have a seat."

"So, how are you?"

"I'm fine. How are you?"

"I'm good."

He looked good, casually dressed. My heart started skipping beats and his eyes had me hypnotized. "Were you dining alone?"

"I was going to order take-out." He said. "I have an early morning flight. I'm going to see my parents."

His cologne smelled good too. "Where is home?"

"Oklahoma."

"Really? My home is Texas."

"For real? What part of Texas?"

"Fort Worth. What part of Oklahoma are you from?"

"Tulsa." He said. "What brought you to New York?"

"I went to NYU and stayed here for law school. I passed the bar the first time and never went back home."

"I went to Howard in D.C. and went to medical school there. I was offered a job here in New York and jumped on it. There was nothing going on back home so, I stayed."

"There was nothing going on back home for me either. But I love New York. I'm so used to it that I wouldn't move back. My only friends are the ones I went to college with, and I barely talk to them. Another close friend of mine lives in Atlanta. We went to high school together and stayed in touch."

We talked and ate together. Andrew was cool and laid back. His wife was crazy to let him go but, I've learned that some women can be as stupid as some men. They would have someone good at home and mess it up trying to play. "Mia contacted me today, again." He said. "She talked to her aunt and threatened to break me if I go forward with the divorce."

"Would you consider a deposition?"

"Sure but, how will that happen? Mia is refusing."

"I'll have her subpoenaed. She will have to show up."

"What will the deposition do?" He asked.

"It is like an interview to gather information to build a case. It will help if we go to trial. But it is possible that we can come to a settlement."

"I doubt that, knowing Mia."

"What would you like for me to do?"

"I'm for that." He said.

"Consider Mia subpoenaed." Andrew paid for our meals and walked me to my car.

"Nice 760." He said.

"Thanks. Is this the H1 your wife wants."

"That's the one." He opened the door for me. "How tall are you?"

"I'm six-feet."

"Wow, that's the second thing I noticed." He said.

"What was the first thing?"

"How beautiful you are."

I smiled. "Thank you."

"You have a good evening, Dina." He said.

"You too. Thanks for dinner. You didn't have to pay for it."

"It was my pleasure."

"Have a safe trip."

"I will." He closed my door and I left.

I smiled during my drive home. Andrew was cool and I was starting to like him more but, I need to remain professional.

Alexis

Chapter 13

It's Monday and I'm off work. Dad was back at home, Jaz is in town with him, and getting MJ settled with Kel. I don't know if she told him about her and Carlin or not. I'm glad she left him. I knew there was something *funny* about him and her so-called friend Denise. Patrick is at work and the boys are at school. I've been thinking about driving out to Winter Hills to find Mom. I have nothing planned today and left.

I went to her neighborhood and drove around, looking for the bricked wall Dad mentioned. The houses here were massive and some people had their expensive cars parked outside. The houses were nice, and the people were friendly.

They were waving, walking their dogs, and some were exercising on their front lawns. Soon, I found the brick wall and drove around to the front gate, hoping I would see her drive out. I drove by slowly and saw her house. It looked like a castle. I circled the wall and cruised the area. I drove back towards the gate and as I got closer, the gate opened. I slowed down and a black Wraith drove out. It was a woman driving and I followed her. That must be Mom.

I followed her to the galleria that had high-end stores. I had no business here. The valet parked her car, and I parked close by. I saw her diamond ring sparkle from the parking garage. I followed her into Robertson's, and she was greeted by her employees after they recognized her. The employees were nice and welcoming. I got a good look at her and noticed how much she and Jaz favored. She was about five-foot-five, curvy, high yellow like Dina, and had layered shoulder length salt and pepper hair. She was casually dressed in jeans, boots, a sweater, and her makeup was flawless. Her fragrance smelled good, and she carried a high-end designer tote.

I followed her around and looked at every item she looked at. She selected a white wool pant suit, a white shirt, and white shoes. I wonder where she's going. I looked at the price tags and they were expensive. Another lady brought out a big white box and she opened it. It was a long white, mink coat. Mom tried it on, and it was glamorous. I then followed her to a jewelry store, and she purchased a huge diamond ring with the matching necklace, bracelet, and earrings. Afterwards, she left and had the valet bring her car around. I hurried to my car and followed her again. She went back home, and I went home.

Later, I cooked dinner and picked up the boys from school. Patrick came home and I couldn't wait to tell him what happened. I hugged and kissed him. We ate and the boys were talking about school. I went in the kitchen and Patrick followed me. "Baby, this food was good." He said.

"Thank you. I need to talk to you too."

"Okay, boys, go do your homework." He shouted. They went to their rooms and Patrick helped me in the kitchen. "What's up?"

"You may think I'm crazy but, I went to Winter Hills to find my mom."

"Did you find her?"

"I think so."

I told him everything she did. I'm surprised he didn't think I was crazy, but I was desperate. "Did you say anything to her?"

"No, I was too nervous to say anything. But I am next time."

"Next time?" He asked.

"You think I'm crazy."

"No, I'm just amazed at how fast you've succeeded. Most people would have to hire someone. You went straight to her. What all did you find out?"

"Jaz looks just like her and shops like her. She's shorter than us, has shoulder length hair, high yellow like Dina, and gorgeous. She was wearing diamonds that sparkled a mile away. She seemed like a sweet person."

"What did she drive?"

"A Rolls Royce Wraith."

"Those are nice." He said. "Next time, say something."

"I don't know what to say but, this stays between us. I don't want to tell Jaz or Dina until I know it's her for sure."

"Baby, you know I'm not going to say anything." He reassured.

The phone rang. "I'll get it. Hello?"

"Hey, it's Jaz."

"What's up?"

"I'm flying back to New York tomorrow. I'm hanging out with Daddy now."

"How is MJ?"

"Excited to be with his dad." She said. "He's all settled."

"How is your divorce going?"

"It's stressing. Dina's working on it, and she filed the legal separation papers. I hate I have to wait a year."

I could hear the depression in her voice. "Jaz, I'm sorry you have to go through all of this."

"Don't be, I'll be fine. You and Patrick hang in there because, this is one feeling that I wouldn't wish on my worst enemy."

"Oh, we're good. You'll get back on your feet. Just be strong. Tell Dina to take you shopping or something."

She laughed. "That sounds like a good idea too. I'll call you before I leave. Y'all have a good night. I'm going to get some sleep."

"Alright. I love you, Jaz."

"Love you too." She said.

"How is she?" Patrick asked.

"She sounds so depressed. Carlin is putting her through it. She caught him in bed with her college friend, moved with Dina, had to send MJ to Kel, our Dad just got out of the hospital, and now have to wait an entire year before she can file for a divorce. The girl is stressed."

"Well, we're stuck with each other." He said. "I knew you were the one when I saw you."

"You almost lost me because you couldn't let go of your ex-girlfriend that you claimed was your *friend*."

"Don't start."

"I'm serious. I was about to leave. I thought you were playing games."

"I wasn't." He said. "I was just taking care of unfinished business so things can be right with us."

Jaz

Chapter 14

I'm flying back to New York later today and I'm on my way to Kel's house to see my son again. He's finishing school here in Texas. I'm going to miss my son. My stay in Texas was bittersweet. I've been getting MJ settled with his dad and he's excited about staying with him. I haven't told Kel everything that what was going on between Carlin and me, but I planned to share this with him eventually. I've been staying with Daddy and keeping my marital issues a secret was challenging. I needed Daddy's advice, but I didn't want him to worry because of his health. I arrived at Kel's house and became nervous when I rang the doorbell. "You're back already?" He asked, opening the door.

I smiled. "Yeah, I just wanted to tell MJ bye before I leave."

"Come on in." I walked in and sat on the sofa. "He's still asleep. I'll wake him up." I looked around the room and walked over to the same pictures I saw back in November.

"I stare at that picture a lot too."

I jumped and Kel stood next to me. "I was just thinking about how much fun we used to have."

He looked at me and I got butterflies. "You were two months pregnant with our son." He said, staring at me.

I couldn't look at him. "Yes. Good memories."

"We can relive them."

"Hi Momma." MJ said, walking in the room, still in his pajamas.

Saved by our son. "Hey, you're sleeping all day?"

"He was up all night, playing video games." Kel said.

"Well, Momma is about to fly back to New York to Aunt Dina's house. I just wanted to say bye."

"Okay."

We hugged and I kissed him on his forehead. "Be good and listen to Daddy, Granny, and Grandpa."

"Okay." He said.

"I love you."

"I love you too."

He walked out of the room. "My mom is excited about him staying with me." Kel said.

"I'm sure she is." Kel was still staring at me, but I couldn't make eye contact. He had that sexy look that always hypnotized me, and he knew it. "Well, I have to go."

I walked to the door, and I felt him on my heels. "Have a safe flight."

I turned around and he was on me. "I will. I'll call when I get to Dina's." He pulled me close to him and kissed me. I kissed him back. *Damn*, this feels good. "What was that for?"

"I've been wanting to do that ever since we split up." He said.

I was speechless. "Okay well, I'll call you later." I left.

I couldn't stop thinking about Kel. I was in a daze driving back to Daddy's house. After Kel laid that kiss on me, I decided to tell Daddy what was going on. I went in the house and Daddy was sitting in the den, reading his newspaper, wrapped in his robe. My bags were packed and sitting by the front door. I stared at Daddy, trying to figure out how to tell him everything that has happened. "What is it, Jaz?" He asked.

"Daddy, I need to talk to you."

He put the newspaper down and removed his reading glasses. "Talk." I told him about me catching Carlin in bed with Denise, the transition to New York, the legal separation, leaving MJ with Kel, and the kiss. "So, when were you going to tell me, Jaz?"

"When you got better. I didn't want to upset you."

"Jaz, I'm fine. You are my daughter. I don't care if I'm on my death bed, you can talk to me about anything. I'm older than you and can handle a lot of things."

"I'm sorry, Daddy. What should I do? What does all this mean? I'm loaded with mixed emotions."

"Jaz, you're vulnerable and having a breakthrough." He said. "I knew something was up with Carlin. I mentioned it to you a few months ago. Now, are you *really* done with Carlin?"

"Yes, I am."

"Well, you're obviously done. You moved your things and MJ's things out the house. Not to mention you shot at him and that girl. Carlin didn't change on you. He revealed who he already was. He was jealous of Kel and married you so Kel wouldn't marry you. It was just a big game to him, and he used his money and lifestyle to win you over Kel. You didn't know what was going on and walked right into it. Kel tolerated him but, he didn't care about him. You knew that."

"Daddy, I was hurt."

"I know, Carlin was your husband." He said. "You were physically and mentally married to Carlin, but your heart and soul was with Kel. It always was. Kel wasn't ready for marriage back then and you hurried to Charlotte and married Carlin."

"Daddy, I wasn't waiting on Kel. He wanted to play games."

"Like I said, he wasn't ready and what you didn't realize was that you weren't ready for marriage either. That didn't mean you had to wait on Kel to be ready, it just meant that you weren't ready. Yes, he was out playing but you were still trying to figure things out with your career, and you both had a son together. That time was for you to figure things out for yourself, and had you waited and focused on that, Kel could have been your husband instead of Carlin."

Daddy had a point. I wasn't ready for a relationship. I was angry with Kel and hoped we could be together back then. "This is a lot."

"It is and Kel wanted you *bad*, he still does." He said. "No, he shouldn't have kissed you, but he couldn't help himself. Although he was wrong, that was confirmation on how you feel about each other. But it's hard for you because you're still legally married to Carlin and have to wait an entire year to file for a divorce." I'm glad I told Daddy. I needed to hear this. "So, for now, just redirect your energy on yourself. Utilize this one year of the legal separation to heal, get yourself established here in Texas, and your son. That's it and don't get caught up with Kel because you're not ready. Dina is helping you, you have our support, and

MJ is safe with his dad. You did the right thing with your son, unlike most mothers."

"Kel is an amazing dad."

"He is. Hang in there. You will be stressed and drained but once this is over, you will be fine, and life will become clear. Be patient and focus on yourself so you can take care of your son. If you still need a place to stay during your legal separation, you can stay here."

"Thank you, Daddy." We hugged and the Uber arrived.

"You're welcome, sweetie. Now hurry so you won't miss your flight and kiss my baby girl for me. Call me when you arrive in New York."

"I will. I love you, Daddy."

"I love you too, baby girl." I left.

I flew to Charlotte first to pick up something I forgot in the house. I didn't tell anyone about me stopping here. I had a car take me to the house and the driver waited for me. I used my key and went inside. Carlin was sitting in the family room and quickly turned around. "Jaz, what are you doing here?" He asked, walking towards me.

"I forgot something."

I walked straight to our bedroom and went to our closet. Carlin followed me, apologizing but I was ignoring him. I grabbed my cherry wooded box and inside was a pistol Daddy gave me when I got married. "What is it with you and guns?" He asked, moving out of my way.

"Well, obviously I needed it."

I walked past him. "Jaz? Will you listen to me?" He yelled.

I turned around. "What Carlin?"

He held up papers. "Have you at least given any thought about us? I was served with legal separation papers."

"Hell no! There is no more *us*! I figured that out when I caught you!"

He took a deep breath and lowered his voice. "Look, I love you Jaz." I shook my head. "Jaz, I want this to work."

"No, you don't! If you did, you would have called me! Trust me, once I walk out that door, Denise will be back on your mind!"

"Look, how is MJ?" He asked, pretending to be concerned.

"Happy! Goodbye!"

"Jaz wait!"

I turned around, frustrated. "What?"

"Just think about this." He begged.

"Carlin, there is nothing to think about. Were you thinking when y'all were having sex in our bed?" He looked off into space. "I didn't think so. Men approach me all the time and I turn them down because I loved you. I was so sure that nothing or no one could tear us apart. But you proved me wrong. Now rather you sign the legal separation agreement or not, I'm not coming back." I walked out and he keep calling my name. I stopped by my storage unit and left my gun there. I planned to have everything transported to Texas once the legal separation is granted. On my way to the airport, my cell phone rang. "What, Carlin?"

"So, it's like that, huh?" He asked, trying to sound tough.

"Yes, it's like that!"

"You want the legal separation, fine! I hope you had a good time being a rich woman because I'm leaving your ass broke!"

I'm back in New York, and Dina and I are talking about Daddy, my stay in Texas, then I told her about my short trip to Charlotte. "Jaz, don't go back over there." She said. "I hope you have everything."

"I do, except for my things in storage. I put my gun in there and arranged to have our things moved to Texas. I donated MJ's bedroom furniture."

"You need to move your things as soon as possible."

"Also, he told me that he was leaving my ass broke and hung up in my face on my way to the airport."

Dina stopped and the color of her face changed. "So, he's threatening you?" She asked.

"Yes."

"We'll see."

"Kel kissed me."

Dina paused. "Now, it's getting interesting. How did you feel?"

"My toes curled!" She laughed. "But this is all too sudden, Dina. I'm still dealing with me and Carlin's separation, and Kel is moving in on me. I'm not ready."

"I understand and I'm sure Kel would." She said. "Just focus on starting over."

Yvette

Chapter 15

Momma is in town and we're taking a road trip to Newport Beach to look at houses. I'm sure she will buy one of them. The doorbell rang and I hurried to the door. "Momma!"

"Hey honey, how are you?" She asked, hugging me.

"I'm fine."

"Good. How is the family?"

"Everyone's fine. Are you ready to go?"

"I'm ready." I locked up my house and we left.

The trip up to Newport Beach was fun. We laughed, talked, and ate. The first house was a two-story house but, Momma thought it was too big. We then went to another house that had an ocean view. She thought it was too small. We went to the last house that had an ocean view but was bigger. "I like this already." She said, getting out the car.

"Good because, this is the last one."

We walked inside and I showed her around. It was a one-story Mediterranean house but big and luxurious. Everything was white, including the exterior of the house. "Do you like it?"

"I love this." She said. "It's not too big and it's not too small. It's perfect. I'll take it."

We went over the paperwork, and she handed me the check. Momma could do that. "I'm glad you like this house. I saved it for last."

"I like the pool too. I think I'm going to put indigo lights in it."

"That will be pretty. I'm going to have the house cleaned and you can move in first of the month."

"Great. Thank you."

"You're welcome."

"Now I have to buy furniture." She said.

I've been tempted to ask her about Daddy but, I didn't want to ruin her moment with the house. She was rambling on about the house and her plans for it, and I interrupted her. "Have you heard from my dad?"

She paused and looked at me. "No." She said. "I'm still trying. He hasn't answered his phone and I've been leaving messages, telling him I had something to tell him. He never called back." We left.

The drive back was long, and I was quiet most of the time, listening to Momma rambling more about the house. We arrived in L.A. and went to my office. I processed her paperwork and she left. I was disappointed about her not hearing from Daddy. I want to meet him, and I had a feeling that this was a dead end and thought about giving up. It was depressing and it made me emotional. I arrived at home and parked in the garage. I went inside and Reggie was in the family room, and Yolanda was upstairs. Reggie greeted me and I hugged him and burst into tears. "Baby, what's wrong?" He asked.

I told him about Momma not hearing from Daddy and me wanting to give up. "I don't know what to do. I don't think I will ever meet him."

"Listen, you will meet him. Be positive, you will meet him. Don't give up, you've come this far."

"Reggie, I'm tired and I have a lot on my mind, finding my dad, making a baby, and opening more offices. Can we do all of this?"

"Yes, baby, we can, and we will." He said. "You are going to find your dad, we're going to keep trying for another baby, and the office is already in works. I know its stressful and scary but, that's what I'm here for. We built this empire together and things can get overwhelming. You can lean on me, baby, I got you." Reggie held me in his arms. "I love you, okay?"

"I love you too."

Dina

Chapter 16

I've been preparing for today's deposition and I'm anxious to see how this goes. Andrew's wife Mia wasn't happy about being subpoenaed and neither was her attorney, Joan Allen. Joan popped up at my office upset about it but, I didn't care. I'm glad Andrew is taking my legal advice. Andrew and I are in the conference room, waiting for Mia and Joan. Andrew seemed nervous but I told him to remain calm, be honest, and not to volunteer extra information if not asked. My assistant Keisha walked Joan and Mia in the conference room and the tension between Andrew and Mia was heavy. Ten minutes into the deposition, things were starting to get a little heated.

"We would like to try to come to a mutual agreement." Joan said.

Mia was looking off into space, rolling her eyes. "I want him to give me the house, his cars, and I'm keeping my car." Mia said.

No she didn't. "If Mr. Hicks agrees to the terms, my client will pay all legal fees and let him have the condo." Joan said.

I couldn't believe this. "No, she can keep her car and the condo, but the Hummer, the Tesla, and the house are mine." He said. "I don't care about the condo. The lease is paid and that will give her time to find a job."

"Well, we'll see." Mia said, with an attitude.

"Mia, that will give you plenty of time to find a job." Andrew said to Mia. "You just don't want to work."

"My client is willing to let her stay in the condo, until the lease expires."

"All of my things are in the house." Mia said.

"My client paid off the lease and it will protect his finances and credit if he remains in the house."

Joan rolled her eyes and Mia was giving me the evil eye. "My client also has a vehicle and would like to keep his cars." Joan said.

"Why does she need all three cars?"

I can't wait to hear this. "Her car has been in and out of the shop with several mechanical issues." Joan handed me the receipts.

"Who paid for the repairs?"

"My mom helped me because Andrew wouldn't." Mia said. "I have nothing!"

"My client needs dependable transportation." Joan said.

Andrew sighed, so sure that this wouldn't go well. "My client refuses to let Mia keep the house and cars. He has caught her with another man in their house."

"That's a lie!" Mia snapped.

"My client shouldn't have to give up anything that he's still paying for."

"Your car is paid for to, Mia." Andrew said. "You're all about money."

"Andrew, I've apologized to you multiple times!" Mia yelled. "I love you and I wanted this to work but you walked out! What am I supposed to do?"

"Get a job, Mia!" Andrew said. "I hope the affair you had was worth it because I'm never taking you back!"

"I'm out of here!" Mia stormed out.

Joan paused. "I guess we'll see you in court." She left.

Andrew and I sat there, speechless. "Okay, this is only round one. Mia walking out made her look bad, and I will bring this up in trial.

"What happens now?" He asked.

"I will meet with Mia's attorney to review the transcript of today's deposition. We'll gather documentation and any evidence provided from both you and Mia to build this case. Mia walking out hurt their case."

"Dina, thank you so much."

"No problem. I need you to get proof of everything because the trial isn't going to be simple. You may have to explain what you saw when you caught her cheating, and if you have any witnesses who are willing to testify, I need to know. I need all financial statements, tax records, assets, liabilities, everything."

"I will be ready. Thank you, Dina."

"You're welcome."

Andrew left and Keisha arrived with lunch. I then began working on Jaz's legal separation. Hers was going to be more work due to all the money and I have to prepare for travel. Soon, Andrew walked in my office. "Andrew? What are you doing here?"

He sat in front of me. "Dina, I want to take you out." He said. "It doesn't have to be a date. I just want to thank you for all you've done."

I thought about it. "Okay Andrew. I'll go out with you."

I gave in. "Cool, how about tonight?"

"Is seven okay?"

"Yes." He said, smiling.

"Okay." I gave him my address and he left.

Its six o'clock and I rushed through the door. "Jaz, I'm home!"

"I'm upstairs!" She shouted. "Are you in a rush?"

"Yes, I have a date and he will be here in an hour." I rushed to my bedroom and Jaz followed me. "I lost track of time at work."

"Wait a minute, what date?"

"Well, not exactly a date but I'm going out with Andrew Hicks."

"Your client?" She asked, surprised. "I can't believe you said yes."

"I had too. He's *fine*, girl."

"I have to meet him. I have to meet the man who is bringing my boring sister out of her shell."

"Very funny. I'm going to take a quick shower. Listen for the door."

After my shower, I applied my make-up and wore my hair down. I put on a multi-colored blouse, black slacks, stilettos, and gold jewelry. I heard the doorbell rang and I was nervous. I sprayed on my favorite perfume and took a final glimpse in the mirror. I could hear Jaz asking him all kinds of questions. I went downstairs and checked him out. He looked *so* fine. "Hey Andrew."

He turned around. "Damn, you look good." He said.

"Thanks. I see you've met my big sister, Jaz."

"Yes, we met." She said. "Now, you two go on and have fun."

"Bye Jaz."

We walked outside and Andrew was the perfect gentleman. He opened the door for me, and his H1 was nice. Our ride to the restaurant was silent. I was nervous and didn't know what to talk about. I just listened to the music and at times, I would feel him staring at me. "You look nice tonight." He said, breaking the silence.

"Thanks. So, do you."

"Are you okay? You're kind of quiet."

"Oh, I'm fine."

I started rubbing my thighs and he stopped me. "Relax, there's no need to be nervous." He said.

He was *so* charming. "Thanks."

We went to a Cajun restaurant and went inside. It was nice but crowded. We were seated and there was a live blues band playing and they sounded good. He ordered us each a glass of wine and I sat back and enjoyed the music. After the band played, we talked. "So, what do you think?" He asked.

"This is nice. I love blues music. How did you know I did?"

"From the pictures on your wall in your office." He said.

"So, you've been paying attention?" He nodded. "All my dad ever listened to was blues. That's what me and my sisters grew up on."

"You have another sister?"

"Yes. She lives in Texas and Jaz just moved here from North Carolina. Alexis is the oldest, then Jaz, and I'm the baby."

"I'm an only child." He said. "I come from a wealthy family and I'm very close to my parents."

"I never knew my mom but, I'm close to my dad."

"You never met your mom?" He asked.

"No. She and my dad broke up after she had me and he raised us."

"That's different. You don't hear that often."

"I know. But we're all close and we still have fun on holidays, although it's just us."

"Do you have any kids?" He asked.

"No. I've never been married but, I have been engaged before."

"What happened with that?"

"He cheated on me and proposed to try to tie me down, basically."

"Wow. I don't have any kids but, I want to have one someday, after I get married again."

"You want to get married again?"

"Of course." He said. "I like married life. Just me and her, whoever she will be."

"I must say, Mia was stupid to let you go. You seem pretty cool."

"I try to be." We ordered our food and continued talking.

My heart has been broken too many times before and I hope that this won't lead to another heartache. Something was telling me to give him a chance. The lights deemed as the band began to play another song. Andrew pulled me close to him and wrapped his arm around me.

We arrived back at my house and Andrew walked me to my front door. "Thanks for everything, Andrew."

"No problem." He said, standing over me. "I'm glad you enjoyed yourself."

"I had so much fun. That's going to be our spot."

"Alright. Well, have a good night."

"You too." He walked off and I stood there, debating if I should kiss him or not. "Andrew?" He turned around. "Can I at least get a hug?"

He laughed. "Sure." He hugged me and I wanted to melt. "Goodnight."

"Goodnight."

I walked in the house and Jaz was standing in the foyer with her arms folded, smiling. "So, how did it go?" She asked.

"It went well. I like him."

Jaz screamed. "Girl, since you and Jason broke up, I didn't think you would give any man a chance."

She followed me upstairs. "Well, Andrew is different. He's patient and he respects me."

"Dina, I have to call everyone I know. This is a dream come true. You went on a date."

"Don't make me get started on you and *Kel*."

"This isn't about me." She said. "This is about you."

I laughed. "Goodnight Jaz." I closed my bedroom door.

"I want details in the morning!" I changed clothes and got in my bed.

I lied there, thinking about Andrew and how much fun I had. It's been a while since I enjoyed the company of a man. He was the perfect gentleman and didn't try anything. I felt guilty also because he's still married and I'm his attorney.

Alexis

Chapter 17

I'm riding through Winter Hills, searching for Mom again. I've been driving around the neighborhood for thirty minutes and there was still no sign of her. Just when I was about to give up, I drove past the gate one last time, and saw a white SUV drive out.

I followed her to an expensive furniture store near downtown and parked close by. She got out her SUV and went inside. I stayed close by and checked out the furniture. I followed her as she picked out several sets of furniture for different rooms. I hope she's not moving. I then overheard her telling her salesman that she wanted everything shipped to Newport Beach, California. I have to say something. She sat on the all-white living room furniture she purchased, and I looked at the price tag. Judging by the price, I could only imagine her house in California. It was made for a mansion. I took a deep breath and walked towards her. "This is beautiful." I didn't know what to say.

"Yes, it is." She said, looking comfortable.

"Did you buy this?"

"Yes, I bought a house in California and I'm having it shipped there."

"What made you move there?"

"Oh, I'm not moving." She said. "I live here in town but, I travel to California often on business. Then I decided to buy a house there. I didn't want to keep crashing at my daughter's house."

We have another sister. "Oh, you don't look old enough to have a daughter with her own house. You're a pretty lady."

She smiled. "Thank you. Please sit with me." I sat next to her, and I took another deep breath. "I'm a grandmother also. My daughter is married, and they have a little girl."

"Really?"

I was getting excited. "Yes. My name is Victoria."

"Hi Victoria, my name is Alexis."

She paused and took a long look at me. "Alexis?" She asked.

"Victoria?" Her salesman called. "Everything is set. I just need you to sign some papers."

"Okay." She said, turning back to me. "Alexis, would you mind waiting here for a few minutes?"

"Not at all." She walked off and I patiently waited.

I was so nervous and excited that I wanted to cry. Soon, she came back. "I'm about to leave." She said. "Were you leaving?"

"Yes, I browsed long enough." We walked outside.

"So, Alexis, are you married?"

"Yes, I am. This is a nice SUV."

"Thank you. Is your maiden name James?"

My heart dropped and my eyes filled with tears. "Yes."

She covered her mouth, in shock and paused. "Oh, my goodness." She said. "Alexis, I'm your mother." She grabbed me and hugged me. We were both in tears and I felt relieved. "Alexis, could you follow me to my house so we can talk?"

"Sure." We left.

I drove up to the gate and her house looked like a palace. There were people working in her yard and cleaning her cars. I parked behind her in front of her house, and we went inside. Her foyer was massive, and she had marbled floors. She had a huge spiral staircase and crystal chandeliers. "Have a seat."

We sat in her family room and the sofa was comfortable. "Would you like something to drink?" She asked.

"I'm fine. This is a beautiful place."

"Thanks. It took a lot of hard work and patience." She stared at me. "How are you, Alexis?"

"I'm fine."

"Thank you for coming over. I'm speechless right now." She was nervous, and I was starting to calm down. I explained the last time I follower her. She laughed. "So, how is Morris?"

"He's not doing well. His diabetes has gotten the best of him. He's been in and out of the hospital but he's home now."

Her eyes got big, and her mouth dropped. "Well, if you don't mind, I would like to see him."

"Sure. He would like that. I remember you saying, back at the store, that you have a daughter."

"Yes. Her name is Yvette. She's married with a ten-year-old daughter named Yolanda. They live in Malibu, and they own a real estate company."

"Wow. Must be nice. Is she tall like us?"

"Yes, she's about five-foot-nine."

"Oh, she and I are the same height."

"Alexis, your dad and I never got married." She said.

"We just had beautiful girls. Morris had a bad attitude towards me but, he was a good dad to y'all. At the time, my mother had just passed, and my dad was ill. He was left to run Robertson's and I was always traveling with him. When you and Jaz were babies, I brought y'all with me but, Morris thought I traveled too much and agreed to keep y'all. Time went on and soon, your dad and I broke up. I found out that I was pregnant three months after we did and never told him. He wouldn't let me keep y'all so, I kept Yvette and moved to California. I went to visit you and Jaz, and your dad and I got back together. I got pregnant with Dina, and we had a long distant relationship. After I had her, I had to get back to work to save the company after my dad passed, and Morris kept Dina. Yvette was all I had."

"Mom, why couldn't you and Dad work this out?"

"Because your dad didn't want to leave Texas and neither did I. While I was in California your dad moved, and I didn't hear from him for years. I got a call from him out of the blue when you were about to get married. I didn't want to pop up after all these years so, I stayed in California. I raised Yvette in Los Angeles, sent her to college, and she later got married. I bought this house and started another business and made Fort Worth the headquarters."

"I'm not upset but I am disappointed."

"I know Alexis but, you have to understand that my family-owned company was in need of work." She said. "I tried to bring y'all with me, but Morris wasn't having it."

"Don't worry Mom. The most important thing is that we found each other."

"I'm so sorry Alexis."

"Mom let's just move on. I love you and I forgive both you and Dad."

She looked at me and smiled. I didn't want to argue with her. I just want to have a mother. "Thank you." She said. "So, tell me about yourself."

"I'm married, and I have two sons, Patrick Jr. and Alexander. They're thirteen and eleven. My husband's name is Patrick and he's a dentist. We live in east Fort Worth and I'm a beautician."

"Oh, you can do my hair." She said.

"Anytime. I've been the only one taking care of Dad because Jaz and Dina live out of state."

"Really?"

"Yes. After high school, I went to beauty school and got my license. Patrick and I are high school sweethearts. Dad liked him and we got married. We had a huge wedding and people still talk about our wedding to this day. Our oldest son is playing basketball and he is the star on the team. He's about to start high school."

"Wonderful! What about the baby?"

"He plays football and they're both honor students."

"Good for them." She said. "How is Jaz?"

"She's doing fine. She's in New York with Dina."

"New York?" She asked.

"Yes. Dina is a lawyer."

"That's good. What about Jaz?"

"She and her husband own a vineyard and dealerships in North Carolina."

"I'd love to meet them."

"I will talk to them."

"I want to keep Yvette a secret." She said. "I'll tell them myself and explain what happened. Your dad doesn't know about Yvette either and I plan to tell him. She recently asked me about him."

"Okay."

"Are you hungry?"

"A little."

"I know of a restaurant where we can have lunch." I rode with Mom in her Wraith.

We ate and talked more. I told her more about myself, my years in school, and my family. I told her about Dad and his current condition. She asked for Dina and Jaz's phone numbers, and I gave them to her. Later, we left and exchanged numbers, and agreed to keep in touch.

I went home, excited, and couldn't wait to tell Patrick. I went inside and took a deep breath. I became emotional, still overwhelmed. Patrick walked up to me and hugged me. "What's wrong?" He asked. "Are you okay?"

"Yes." He sent the boys to their rooms. "I'm just in shock right now."

"What's wrong?"

"I met my mom."

Jaz

Chapter 18

I flew to Texas again to see MJ and Daddy. I enjoy living with Dina and we hang out a lot. I liked New York but I was ready to move back to Texas. I talk to MJ almost every day and he's happy with his dad. I'm staying with Daddy, and I'm glad I told him about my divorce, and he gave good advice. I've been focused on my legal separation, and I haven't heard from Denise or Carlin. Carlin was my husband and he betrayed me, but Kel was my high school sweetheart and gave me our son. That kiss made everything confusing. Alexis called and told me that she had something to tell me. She sounded as if everything was okay, but I was concerned, and she wanted me to come over.

I arrived at Alexis' house in Daddy's Cadillac. I went inside and she seemed normal but was up to something. After I walked in, a Maserati parked next to me. She opened the door and a woman, who was well dressed and covered in diamonds, walked in. I walked over to her. "Hi, I'm Jaz."

"Hello Jaz, I'm Victoria."

I paused. "Really? That's my mother's name."

Alexis laughed and I was confused. "Jaz, this is Mom."

I stopped and took a long look at her. It was like looking in a mirror. My heart was racing, and my eyes filled with tears. "Momma?"

She opened her arms, and I hugged her. "It's me, baby." She said. "Oh Jazmine, you're so gorgeous."

"So are you. I can't believe this. Alexis, you had me thinking something was wrong."

She laughed. "No, I found our mother."

"I have to call Dina."

"No!" She said. "Mom wants to surprise her."

"Okay. She will be surprised. Wow."

"I'm going to let you two talk." She said. "I'll be in the other room."

"Thanks Alexis." She walked off.

I sat down, still staring at Momma. She got up and sat next to me. "So, how have you been Jaz?" She asked, looking at my oversized cherry red afro.

"I've been fine. I'm so happy to finally meet you."

"Me too. You have a lot of hair. I love it." She explained how Daddy ended up raising us and her running a family-owned business. Momma was banking, and I've shopped at her store. She and I were alike and had a lot in common. I loosened up and we had a long conversation. "Tell me about you."

"After high school, I went to college in North Carolina. I got my MBA in Business and met my now husband, Carlin. I came back home for a while and ran into my high school sweetheart. He and I started dating again and I got pregnant. I have a son named Markell Jr., we call him MJ, and he's in town with is dad."

"Aw, I bet he's handsome. How old is he?"

"He's ten. After I had MJ, I was offered a job in Charlotte. MJ's dad and I were having problems and I left and took our son with me. Carlin and I found each other, and he was shocked that I had a son. We hooked back up and at the time, he had taken over his dad's dealerships in North Carolina. We got married, me and MJ moved in with him in Charlotte, and later opened a vineyard there. I manage them and he manages the auto dealerships."

"Wow, you've been doing good." She said, impressed.

"Yes. I flew down here to check on Daddy and when MJ and I got home, I caught my husband in bed with my best friend from college." Momma gasped. "I packed our things, sent MJ here with his dad, and I moved with Dina in New York."

"I'm sorry to hear that."

"Oh, don't be. I'm okay. Dina is my lawyer."

"Good." She said. "There is something else that I want to share with you. Y'all have another sister. Morris doesn't know about her. I had her between you and Dina."

"We do?"

"Yes." Momma told me all about her and that she was going to bring us together. "I understand if you're upset."

"No, I'm not. Don't think that. I'm just shocked."

It's Thursday and I'm flying to Charlotte today for court. Dina is meeting me there. I was still thinking about Momma and how successful Alexis was finding her. She and I bonded instantly, and she was so beautiful. I did look like her and I wondered if our other sister was tall like us. I can't wait to meet her, and I was anxious to see the look on Dina's face when she meets Momma. It was hard keeping Momma a secret from Daddy. I don't know when Alexis is going to tell him. After I packed, I went to Kel's house. "Hey Jaz." He said, opening the door.

"Hey, I'm about to fly to Charlotte for court."

"Okay, I'll get MJ."

MJ came out and I hugged him and said my goodbyes. I miss my son. He went back in the room and Kel gave me a strange look. "Well, I better go."

"No, something is wrong." He said. "What's up?"

"You could always read me."

"I know. Now what's wrong?"

"Kel, I met my mom yesterday for the first time."

He raised his eyebrows. "What was she like?" He asked.

"She was cool. She's gorgeous and very rich."

"Rich?"

"Yes. She has a family-owned business called Robertson's."

"Robertson's the department store?"

"Yes."

"Whoa! That's a surprise." He said.

"Yes, it is and I'm still in shock. We exchanged numbers and we're going to keep in touch. She also told me that we have another sister."

"For real?"

"Look, I'm sorry to rush but, I have a flight to catch."

He walked me to the door. "No problem." He said. "Call me if you want to talk."

"I will. Thanks." He gave me a long warm hug. "Bye."

I arrived in Charlotte and met Dina at a hotel. We checked into the penthouse and went to the room. "Jaz, you didn't have to get a penthouse." Dina said.

"You know how I am."

My mind was still on Momma. "Are you okay? You've been acting like something is on your mind."

"I'm fine, just nervous."

"Don't be. Now, let's go."

We're sitting in the courtroom and Carlin was sitting on the other side with his attorney, ignoring me. Carlin wanted the house, the dealerships, the vineyard, and stores. He was only going to leave me with my car. He had a high dollar lawyer with him. I've never seen Dina work her magic in the courtroom but, hopefully she will get me *something* out of this. Carlin's attorney was Dan Payton, an attorney whom Dina had heard of but never faced in court.

We stood when the judge walked out and took our seats. Dina told the judge everything about me catching Carlin in bed with another woman. "Your honor, she shot at her." Carlin said.

"Mr. Lawrence, you will get your turn!" The judge yelled. "Miss. James?"

"Your honor, the mistress refused to leave the house after my client caught them in bed together." Dina said. "He even refused to leave, and my client was forced to leave the house with her son."

"Why did you put her out, Mr. Lawrence?" The judge asked.

"Because I had nowhere to go." Carlin said. "She has sisters everywhere that she could stay with."

"Your honor, my client has every right to stay in that house." Dan said, handing the bailiff documents to give to the judge. "This is proof that he was the only one providing for the house and it was his before they were married."

The judge looked at them and looked at me. "Mrs. Lawrence, do you have a place to stay at the moment?" She asked.

"Yes ma'am."

"Did you get everything you wanted out of the house?"

"I have all of my things, but he has all the furniture. I have my car also."

"Which is…?"

"The Mercedes."

"Okay. Mr. Lawrence, what all do you have?"

"I have everything else, your honor." Carlin said. "I also want a restraining order against her."

No he didn't. "Why?" The judge asked.

"Because I don't want her shooting up my house like she did the last time. I don't want her around my businesses either."

"Okay, I've looked over the separation agreement and Mr. Lawrence, you want the dealership and the vineyard. Mrs. Lawrence, you also want the vineyard, is that correct?"

"Yes, your honor."

"Will you be living in the state of North Carolina?"

"No, your honor."

"How do you plan to manage the vineyard in another state?" The judge asked.

"I will be traveling. I can handle it. I've been managing the vineyard and stores."

"Your honor, clearly Mrs. Lawrence won't always be available to manage the vineyard or stores living in another state." Dan said. "My client wishes to continue managing the vineyard and stores as well as the dealerships."

"Very well." The judge said. I wanted to cry. "Anything else?"

"Yes, your honor." Dina said. "With Mr. Lawrence managing the vineyard and stores, as well as the dealerships, which will hinder my clients' finances, my client wishes to have temporary alimony during their legal separation."

"Thank you." The judge said. "My judgement will go as follows – Mr. Lawrence will continue to manage the auto dealerships and the vineyard and stores. He will remain in the house and will keep the Land Rover Range Rover, Rolls Royce Ghost, Ferrari 488 Italia, and the Porsche Panamera. Mrs. Lawrence is restrained from the house and the businesses during the one-year separation. She will keep the Mercedes-Benz S550, Bentley Continental GT, Cadillac Escalade, and will receive temporary alimony of eight thousand dollars per month." The judge banged her gavel.

I was pissed and Carlin walked out with a smile on his face. "Don't give up Jaz." Dina said. "Let's get your Bentley and Escalade and take them back to the penthouse."

We're now in the penthouse, discussing what happened. "I can't believe this. I had plans for that vineyard."

"Jaz, listen to me." Dina said. "This will sound crazy to you, but I need you to trust me on this. I think this is good for you."

"How Dina? He got everything!"

"Jaz, Carlin set himself up for failure. You and I both know that he can't manage that vineyard or the stores. He knows that too."

Dina had a smirk on her face. "So, you backed down on purpose?"

"That's right. I researched the financial history of your vineyard while he was running it in the beginning, and it wasn't doing well. The numbers were bad, and you almost lost it. When you took over, it grew and then you opened the stores. It was down when he ran it and growing when you did. I need proof of everything. I need the contracts on the companies, all assets, and liabilities so I can get you what you deserve. I will be monitoring the vineyard and stores during your separation."

"What am I supposed to do?"

"Rest." She said. "Don't think about the vineyard, let him stress himself out while you enjoy the eight grand you'll be receiving every month."

I smiled. I liked Dina's plan. "I get it now. I'm going to hang out with Daddy and my son. But when it's time for the divorce, I want the vineyard and stores back."

"No problem."

I was frustrated. I wanted the vineyard and stores. I managed them. All Carlin cared about was the dealerships. I wanted to cry but I had to hold it together. Relocating and getting everything transferred was expensive and the alimony is all I'll have. I wanted to buy a house near my son so he can be close to his dad and me. I planned to have my items in storage transported to Texas when I get my house, and have my cars transported. I'm going to get all the information Dina needs. Carlin had a lot more money and he was trying to keep it all. I will get what I deserve.

Yvette

Chapter 19

I'm on my way to Newport Beach to meet Momma at her new house. She's excited about her new home and invited me to go shopping with her. I hope she has some news for me about Daddy. If not, I'm going to hire someone to find him. I arrived at her new home and rang the doorbell. "Hey honey, how are you?" She asked.

"I'm fine, how are you?"

"Great, come on in." Her house was still empty, and we sat on the kitchen counter tops. "The furniture is on the way now. How are Reggie and Yolanda?"

"They're fine. School is out and they're having fun in the swimming pool. Have you filled up your garages yet?"

"Not yet." She said. "I'm just going to buy one car."

Soon, we heard a truck outside. Momma opened the door and the delivery guys brought in her furniture. It was beautiful and all white. After the delivery guys left, we talked more in the family room. "So, how long will you be here?"

"I'll be here until next week, finishing up the house." She said. "Now, let's go shopping."

We went to the mall, outlet stores, and ate lunch. Momma bought bedding, decorations, kitchen items, and greenery. We dropped off everything at her house and she decided to purchase a new car. Momma wrote a check for an SUV and we dropped my car off at her house. I hopped in her new SUV and we continued shopping. Momma bought all her electronics and everything else for her house, including outdoor furniture for the lanai. We went back to her house and relaxed. We were both exhausted and sat on her lanai, enjoying her view of the beach. "You know, I never thought I would say this but, I'm tired of shopping."

She laughed. "I hear you. What time were you heading back?"

"In an hour. I want to get there before dark, so Reggie won't be worried." Momma sat there, staring at the beach in a daze. "Momma, are you okay?"

"Oh, I'm okay." She said, hesitating.

"Momma, what's wrong?"

She turned to me. "Yvette, I have something to share with you before you go."

"Is everything okay?"

"Everything is fine." She said. "A few weeks ago, shortly after I bought this house, I was followed by a young woman to the furniture store. She sat with me, and we started talking. I thought she was pretty, and she looked familiar. I introduced myself and she told me her name. My heart dropped and I asked her to wait while I sign papers for the furniture. We walked outside and I asked what her maiden name was. When she said it, I knew it was her."

"Who was she?"

Momma looked at me. "My daughter."

My mouth dropped. "Your daughter?"

"Yes baby."

"I have a sister?"

"Yes." She said. "Her name is Alexis and she's the oldest."

"How old is she?"

"Thirty-eight."

I didn't know how to react. "Do I have any other sisters?"

"You have two more."

"Two more?"

"Jazmine and La'Dina." She said. "Jaz is thirty-five and Dina is thirty-one."

"So, I'm in the middle?"

"Yes."

"What about my dad?"

Momma took a deep breath. "I found him." My heart started racing. "He's in Fort Worth, Texas and we talked. I haven't told him about you yet. He's been sick and I didn't want to excite him but I'm going to tell him. Yvette, I'm so sorry." She said, getting emotional.

"I have to see him. Do any of them know about me?"

"Only Alexis and Jaz. I told them that I wanted to tell Dina myself. I haven't met her yet. I'm flying to New York to meet her next week."

"When will I get to meet them?"

"After I meet Dina."

I was still trying to wrap my head around everything she told me. "Can you tell me about them?"

"Your dad is retired from the post office. He's diabetic and just got out of the hospital after suffering a stroke. He's at home now and doing better. I haven't seen him, but we talked on the phone. Alexis is a beautician, she's married with two boys, and she lives in east Fort Worth, near your dad. Jaz is going through a divorce, she has a son by her ex from high school, and she lived in Charlotte, North Carolina. Dina is an attorney in New York."

"Who do they look like?"

"Alexis looks like a combination of me and your dad, Jaz looks just like me, but I haven't seen Dina." She said. "You and Alexis are the same height and Jaz is a little shorter than y'all. Morris is tall."

"Who do I look like?"

"Your dad."

I couldn't believe this. I had mixed emotions and hid my anger. I was just happy to have sisters and glad that she found Daddy. "I want to meet him."

"Okay. As soon as I reunite with Dina, I'll let you know. I want you, Reggie, and Yolanda to fly down to my house in Texas."

"Okay, I better get going." She walked me to the door. "I'll call you when I get home."

"Thanks for not being upset."

"Sure. I love you, Momma."

"I love you too." I left.

I cried on and off all the way home. Deep down, I was angry with Momma and wanted to go off. How could she not wonder where her own children were? Why didn't she at least tell me that I had sisters? This should have been the first thing she said before shopping. I'm going to keep my cool and meet my sisters and Daddy.

I arrived at home and went inside. Yolanda hugged me and she went upstairs to her room. I went to our bedroom and Reggie followed me. He could tell something was wrong. "Are you okay?" He asked. I couldn't talk. I reached for him and hugged him, in tears. "Baby, what's wrong?"

I finally calmed down and told him what all Momma found out and my feelings towards her. "I don't know how to feel."

"Listen, your mom should have told you about them, you're right about that. You have every right to be upset too. But she's still your mother. For now, just focus on meeting your family. I'll be there beside you."

Dina

Chapter 20

Jaz and I are sitting in my living room, laughing, listening to music, and talking. I opened a bottle of wine, and we were getting buzzed. She's been enjoying New York and I'm going to miss her when she moves back to Texas. I wanted to give her more in court but, the judge was trying to keep things brief, and Jaz needs to focus on herself and her son. Plus, I wanted to feel Carlin's attorney out. I got Jaz more than usual in alimony but, I have plans for the divorce. She had enough money to get back on her feet and start over back home. I often wondered if she and Kel would get back together but, it's too soon. She was confused but her heart was always with Kel. "So, have you tried getting back with Kel?"

"I thought about it but, I want to get myself together first. Plus, I'm still married."

"I understand but I can tell you still like him."

"It's no different than you liking Andrew."

"Why did you have to go there?"

"Because it's true." She said.

"He is fine."

She started laughing. "See what I mean?"

"Have you told Kel what's going on?"

"No and he's been asking." She said.

"Call him."

"For what?"

"Jaz, you don't have to go into detail but, at least let him know why you're moving back to Texas. Call him."

Jaz dialed his number and put the phone on speaker. I sat quietly and listened. "Hello?" He answered.

"Hey, it's Jaz." She said, looking nervous.

"What's up?"

"Nothing. How is MJ?"

"He's good." He said. "He and Donnie's kids are spending the night at my mom's house."

My doorbell rang and I ran to answer it while Jaz continued her conversation. I opened the door and there was a woman standing there, dressed up and covered in diamonds. "Hi, can I help you?"

"Yes, I'm looking for Jaz." She said. "Is she here?"

"Yes, come on in. I'm her little sister, Dina."

"Hi Dina, I'm Victoria." She said.

"Nice to meet you." *Victoria?* We walked in the living room and Jaz was just hanging up with Kel. "Jaz, you have company."

"Hi, I'm glad you could make it." Jaz said.

"Me too." Victoria said.

"Have a seat."

They sat next to each other. "So, how do y'all know each other?"

"Dina, you may want to sit for this." Jaz said.

I sat across from them and noticed how much they favored. "What's up?"

"Dina, this is our mother." Jaz said.

My heart started racing and my mouth dropped. "Our mother?"

"Yes."

I was speechless and my eyes filled with tears. Momma stood and walked over to me. I couldn't move. She hugged me and cried. Jaz smiled.

"I'm going to go upstairs and talk to Kel." Jaz walked off.

"Oh Dina, you are so beautiful." She said.

"So are you. I can't believe this. I knew your name sounded familiar. How did you find me?"

"Jaz told me where you were. I told her that I wanted to surprise you."

"You did."

Momma told me all about herself and her businesses. She told me about Daddy wanting to keep us and how she was always traveling. Then she told me that we had another sister in California who knows about us. "So, tell me about yourself." She said.

"After I graduated high school, I attended NYU on a scholarship and went to law school after I graduated. I passed the bar the first time and now I'm an attorney. I have a small practice in Manhattan, I moved in a condo there, and I just bought this brownstone. I've never been married, and I have no kids. I do have a friend. His name is Andrew and he's a surgeon."

"Oh, nice." She said. "All of you turned out successful. I see you're the tallest. How tall are you?"

"I'm six-feet tall. I get that a lot."

"Dina, I'm sorry for not being there all of these years." She said.

"Don't be, Momma. I'm just glad we finally met."

"Me too." I hugged her again. "Yvette is flying to Texas so everyone can meet each other. I'd like for you to come. Jaz and Alexis agreed to be there."

"I will be there."

"Good. Also, your dad knows I've met Alexis and Jaz, and that I was coming here to meet you. He doesn't know about Yvette yet." I nodded. "Oh Dina, you have no idea how happy I am."

"Me too. This is different." Momma and I talked more, and she later left.

Jaz and I talked for a while about Momma and all of us meeting. She looked gorgeous, and was humble. Jaz then told me about her conversation with Kel. "We decided to be friends." She said.

"Good, MJ will be happy."

"Yes, he will. This has been an interesting year. First, Daddy goes in the hospital, Carlin cheats on me, and we met our mother."

"What's next? Never mind, I don't want to know." Meeting Momma was exciting but, I didn't know if I should be upset with her or not. I then decided to call Daddy. "Hi Daddy."

"Hey Dina, how are you?" He asked.

I was happy to hear his voice. I told him about Momma being here and he was glad that we finally met her. "Daddy, I have mixed feelings about this."

"Listen, you have every right to be upset, if you are. But keep in mind that she is still your mother. I want you all to get to know each other and bond. Your momma and I have been communicating, and we get along just fine. We buried the past and we're moving forward."

I remembered Momma mentioning that Daddy didn't know about our other sister. I never mentioned her to him. I don't know how Daddy will react when he finds out about Yvette but I'm excited to meet her. I then told Daddy about Andrew. I was hesitant on telling him and decided to for his input. "Daddy, am I wrong?"

He chuckled. "Dina, he's still legally married." He said. "Do you have to ask that question?" He was right. "You're a grown woman and you're going to do what you want but, be careful. He's vulnerable, rather he admits it or not. You're an attractive woman and men look at you. You caught his eye, and he went for it. Be his friend and nothing else."

Alexis

Chapter 21

Dina and Jaz are in town and we're meeting our sister Yvette at Mom's house. I'm anxious to meet her. I wonder if she looks like us, Mom, or Dad. I'm the strong one, Jaz is the party girl, and Dina is the bookworm. Jaz has Dad's temper when she's mad. Maybe Yvette is like Dad also. Dad still doesn't know about Yvette, and I don't know how he will feel when he finds out that he has another daughter. I think he will be thrilled but upset with Mom for keeping her away from him, and I wouldn't blame him.

I wore a maxi dress, sandals, and my hair was up in a bun. I put on my large hoop earrings, applied my makeup, eyelashes, and sprayed on my perfume. After we got dressed, my sisters came over and we followed each other to Mom's house. I was nervous and excited. This was all I've been talking about since I met Mom.

We drove around to her front door and parked. "This is a damn palace!" Jaz said.

"Do you have to be so loud, Jaz?"

"I'm sorry but, this is huge." She said, still being loud.

"Let's go inside." Dina said.

Mom's butler escorted us to the family room, and we waited for Mom to come out. Jaz brought MJ, and Dina came alone. I had my family with me, and I brought a photo album from Dad's house to show our sister.

"Hello everyone." Mom said, walking around the corner. She looked gorgeous as usual. "I'd like y'all to meet your sister, Yvette." She said.

Yvette walked in the room and our mouths dropped. She was so beautiful and favored Dad. She was my height, slim but curvy, dark skinned, had a round baby face, and had a bob haircut. Her husband was very handsome and looked like a model, and their daughter was adorable. Mom introduced us to her, one by one, and everyone was in tears.

"I'd like y'all to meet my husband, Reggie." Yvette said. We all hugged and shook hands. "This is our ten-year-old daughter, Yolanda."

"She favors Jaz." Dina said.

We talked for a while and got to know each other. I showed Yvette our photo album and she showed us hers. We shared stories about Dad raising us and our lifestyle. Our lifestyle was different from hers. We grew up in the hood and I was the first one to move out when I got my cosmetology license. Jaz moved away to college and later, Dina left for college. Yvette was brought up in a wealthy neighborhood but attended a public school. She was down to earth, and I could tell she had Dad's temper. She and Jaz together could be dangerous.

Mom had food delivered for us and we ate together. Yvette was cool and sassy. Although we just met her, the love was strong, and our husbands bonded. We hung out all day and the kids played with each other. I wanted to talk to Mom about Yvette and Dad meeting. I saw her walk in the kitchen and went to talk to her. "Hey Mom, do you need help?"

"No honey, I got it." She said. "I really appreciate you all coming over. My house is always opened to you all."

"Thank you. When do you plan to tell Dad about Yvette?"

"I'm going to talk to Yvette first and go talk to your dad. I don't want to excite him but, he needs to know about her. She is anxious to meet him."

"If you want, I can be there when you tell Dad."

"I'd like that." She said. "Thank you again, Alexis. Let's do this tomorrow."

I'm at Dad's house and he was sitting in the den, watching TV. He was doing better, and I was glad he was finally listening to the doctor. Jaz and Dina were out with Yvette, and I was meeting up with them later. I told Dad that Mom wanted to talk to him. He was opened to her coming over and I gave her his address. Dad was calm about Mom being around again but, I don't know what he's thinking. "Dad, how do you feel about Mom being around again?"

He removed his reading glasses. "Alexis, your momma and I are done." He said. "She and I are not getting back together. I admit that she was the love of my life but, that was then. She's doing her thing and I'm doing mine. I'm just glad that you found her."

"Me too. Jaz looks just like her."

"Yes, she does."

I heard a car door and looked out the window. It was Mom in her luxury SUV. I met her at the door and hugged her. She was casually dressed yet glamorous. She and Dad hugged, and she sat across from him. They had small talk and I sat in the dining room, listening. They were getting along well and laughed, but I was nervous for Dad. "Morris, I need to talk to you about something." Mom said.

"What's that, Vickie?" He asked, giving her his undivided attention.

"When we broke up after I had Jaz, I moved to California to expand Robertson's." I had butterflies and was looking at Dad. "About two months after we broke up, I found out that

I was pregnant." Dad nodded, still looking at Mom. "I had another daughter and never said anything."

"Is she mine?" He asked.

Mom's eyes filled with tears, and I became emotional. "Yes." She softly said. "Morris, I'm so sorry."

Dad sighed while rubbing his face, trying to ponder what she told him. I couldn't tell if he was angry or not. "Why didn't you tell me, Vickie?"

"Because you kept Alexis and Jaz from me."

"Vickie don't put this on me. You and I both knew that your work came first."

"Morris, I just lost my dad at the time, and I had to keep the company going." She said.

"Let's make one thing clear, Vickie." He said, getting upset. "I didn't take our daughters away from you. I got custody and you had visitation rights because you were moving around and traveling a lot. I wasn't going to let you put our daughters through that. I was more stable. I was thinking about them, and you could have come to see them whenever you wanted too. But you didn't."

Mom nodded, looking down. "You're right and I'm sorry, Morris. I admit that I was wrong for that but, I'm here now. They're grown and I missed out on everything but, you have another daughter."

"You kept her a secret while carrying Dina?" Mom began to cry again. "Vickie, that was low. We got back together, you got pregnant with Dina, and you never told me about her. Why?"

"Because I kept her a secret for so long and was too afraid to say anything. Then, you took Dina."

"There you go again, Vickie!"

"Morris, she was all I had!" Mom shouted. "I'm sorry, that's all I can say!"

"Dad, she wants to meet you."

Dad paused, trying to calm down. I could tell he was angry with Mom, and she was still in tears. "What is her name? Where is she? I want to meet my daughter."

Mom finally stopped crying. "Her name is Yvette and she's flying back to Malibu. I'll let her tell you about herself when you meet."

"You do that, Vickie."

Mom stood. "Morris, I'm sorry." She said. Dad just looked at her, disappointed. "I'm going to pay for this for the rest of my life. I'll tell Yvette that you know about her."

"I want to meet my daughter."

"I'll let her know. I'm sorry again and thank you for raising our daughters. You should be proud."

"Trust me, I am." Dad was pissed.

I walked Mom outside. "I'm speechless."

"Your dad has every right to be mad at me, Alexis." She said. "Thank you for being here."

"No problem. Talk to you soon." We hugged and she left. I went back inside, and Dad had tears in his eyes. This hurt me and I hugged him. "Dad, I'm so sorry."

"Don't be, it's not your fault." He said. "I just want to meet my daughter."

Jaz

Chapter 22

Dina flew back to New York, I stayed in Texas with Daddy, and Yvette and I have been hanging out. We talked about her businesses, and I told her about my divorce, and me moving back to Texas. She and I were so much alike. We're at Momma's house browsing her website for houses. I plan to buy a house from her soon. "What areas are your houses here in?"

"I have twenty houses in Dallas and ten in Fort Worth." She said.

"I want to move to Fort Worth."

"I have two in Winter Hills by Momma, one is further out west, just outside the city limits on acres of land. Two are north of the city, three are in Mount Vista, and the other two are in east Fort Worth."

"I want to look at the one with the acres of land and the ones in Mount Vista."

She showed me the house with the acres of land. I watched the virtual tour video, and I liked it but, it was too big. We then looked at the houses in Mount Vista. I looked at two of the three houses, but they were plain. As soon as I saw the last house, I knew it was the one. "This one is a one story and it's big, but you will love it." She said.

"I love it already." I checked out the photos and it was just my style. "How many garages does it have?"

"Four." She said. "This house is one of the top ten that has been shown the most."

"Why hasn't anyone bought it?"

"People are still bidding on it."

"I'll bid on it."

"Okay, I'll put your bid in." She said. "If I don't hear from anyone soon, it's yours."

"Hopefully, it will be available. Carlin is only paying me eight grand a month in alimony."

"If someone outbids you, we can always build one like it. We work with builders as well."

"But I like this community." I changed my mind. "I'm going to wait."

"What all have you done with the money?"

"I bought MJ new clothes, I've invested in stocks, and the rest is sitting in the bank. I've registered my cars here in Texas and I received my Texas driver's license. I'm using Daddy's address. I never thought that Carlin could be such an asshole. I don't know what's going on with that vineyard."

Yvette could tell that I was getting frustrated. "Jaz, relax." She said. "Just be cool. Carlin will get what's coming to him. I'm sure Dina is working hard on your case."

"She is. I wasn't prepared but, I am now."

"Good. Look on the bright side, Kel is here for you."

He has been supportive. "He is a good man. I can't believe we never made it."

"Things happen for a reason. You'll find out why as time goes."

I hope Dina will get me what I deserve. I'm ready to start over. I'm still living with Dina in New York, hoping to buy a house in here in Texas before I move. I had my Bentley and Escalade transported here. The Bentley was at Momma's house, and I kept the Escalade at Daddy's. My Benz was still in New York. Daddy was doing better, and I was glad that Momma finally told him about Yvette. Yvette planned to meet him before she flies back home.

Yvette and Reggie took Yolanda out to eat and they were going to Alexis' house afterwards. I decided to go visit my son and left. I missed my son more than anything. I arrived at Kel's house and rang the doorbell and as usual, I became nervous. "Hey, come on in." He said, opening the door. "Is that your Escalade?"

"Yes, I had it transported here."

"That's nice!" He said, checking it out.

Kel was wearing jeans, a t-shirt, and sneakers. He looked good as always and I kept my composure. I visited with him and MJ and planned to take my son to see Daddy tomorrow. He was enjoying being with his dad and his side of the family. Kel has been very supportive with Daddy, and I was grateful for that. He and I always got along but it was rough after our break-up. Kel had a tremendous heart but had no problem cussing someone out. He was an alfa-male and very dominate. What he said went and people knew not to cross him.

As we were visiting, I found myself staring at him. He was *so* good looking to me. It was something about the way he talked, his laughter, his smile, and the comforting sound of his voice. I loved the relationship he had with MJ and although MJ favored me, he had Kel's personality. After visiting, I got ready to leave. I hugged and kissed my son, and he went back to his bedroom. Kel followed me to the door. "Thanks again for keeping MJ. He is crazy about you."

"No problem, Jaz." He said, standing over me. "He's our son and you know I will do anything for him."

"I know. I'll be flying back to New York soon to get the rest of my things and move with my Dad. Yvette showed me a house earlier but, I can't get it right now."

"Jaz, something better will come along. Be patient and be thankful for what you already got out of him. If you insist on having your own place, rent for now."

He was right, as always. I wasn't broke but, I had plans. I hope I get the vineyard and stores. I'm willing to let go of everything else. "I may consider that. Thank you for everything, Kel."

"No problem." He said. "I'll see you tomorrow."

I wanted a hug, but he backed away. It hurt but, he and I are just friends. I left.

Yvette

Chapter 23

It's been two weeks since I met my sisters, and they are so beautiful. We bonded and got along well, but Dina didn't stay long. I planned to fly to New York to hang out with her soon. Alexis was cool and nurturing, and I loved her style. Jaz was a lot of fun and we bonded instantly. She was very pretty and had so much hair. Dina was fun as well but, her work came first, and she is the tallest. It felt nice to have siblings and Yolanda developed a brother sister relationship with her cousins. Reggie got along with Patrick, and maybe we'll meet Kel and Dina's new friend one day. Momma told me about her conversation with Daddy. They had an argument, but he wanted to meet me. I want to meet him but didn't know when. Since they had an argument, I decided to lay low until the smoke clears. Alexis filled me in as well. She said Daddy was pissed with Momma and I didn't blame him. I was still mad at her as well.

Reggie was upstairs tucking in Yolanda and I'm in our bathroom, taking a pregnancy test. I took one before we went to Texas, and I wanted to take another one. My doctor's appointment is tomorrow but I didn't tell Reggie. I let it sit for a few minutes and keep a look out for Reggie. I heard his footsteps and ran to look at the results and trashed it. "Yvette?" He called.

"I'm in the bathroom. Is Yolanda asleep?"

I walked out. "Halfway." He said, changing his clothes.

"I'm going to sit out on the loggia."

I sat and watched the waves hit the beach. The moonlight shined perfectly over the water and the breeze felt nice. Reggie joined me and we sat in silence. I was thinking about Daddy. "What's wrong?" He asked.

"Nothing."

"Yvette, you're thinking about something." He said.

"I was just thinking about my dad. I want to meet him."

"Why don't you go? You should talk to him and get to know him. Take the jet tomorrow."

"I just may go and take Yolanda with me. What are you going to do while we're gone?"

"I'll be at the office." He said. "I may have to go to Sacramento to show a house, if they call."

"I forgot about that."

"Don't worry. I'll take care of it."

Soon, I got sleepy and was ready to go to bed. "I'm going to bed."

He followed me inside. "You sure have been sleeping a lot."

Yolanda and I just landed in Texas. I talked to Momma last night and told her we were coming today. She told me she was going to talk to Daddy. Yolanda and I stopped at my doctor's office right before leaving and I'm two months pregnant, and due in January. I can't wait to tell Reggie. He's going to be so excited. We took an Uber to Momma's house, and she was happy to see us. "How is Daddy?"

"He's doing much better." She said, sipping her coffee. "He's excited to meet you."

"I'm going to see him later. I'm going upstairs to take a nap."

I stood up and stretched. "Are you okay?" She asked. "You look different but, I can't put my finger on it."

"I'm fine. Yolanda and I had a long flight."

"Okay, I have some errands to run. I'll bring Yolanda with me."

It's six o'clock in the evening and I couldn't believe I slept for four hours. I got up, took a shower, and got dressed. I called Alexis and told her that I was in town and was going to meet Daddy. She was meeting me there. Momma and Yolanda were still gone, and I took one of Momma's cars to see Daddy.

I parked next to Alexis' car, and I was nervous. I took a deep breath and Alexis walked outside. "Hey, how are you?" She asked, hugging me.

Alexis looked pretty, as always. She was casually dressed in skinny jeans, sneakers, and a bright colored top. "I'm fine, how are you?"

"I'm great. You look good!"

"You do too. I love your style. Is Daddy ready?"

"Yes, are you okay?" She asked.

I took a deep breath. "Yes. Yolanda is with Momma. I'll bring her over before we leave."

"Okay, let's go in." I followed her inside.

I looked around and Daddy had a small and cozy house. His den had a huge, bricked wood burning fireplace. Across from it was the dining room and the front windows were big. The house was old, but it had a lot of character.

Alexis went to get Daddy and I waited in the den. Butterflies filled my stomach, and he walked in the den. He was tall, skinny, and had a cane. I smiled and tears immediately filled my eyes. He smiled when he saw me, and I ran to hug him. We were both in tears and I immediately felt the father daughter love between us. We hugged for a long time and repeatedly said *'I love you'* to each other.

Alexis left and Daddy and I talked. Daddy was a comedian. He made me feel comfortable and I felt like I could talk to him about anything. "Where do you live?" He asked.

"I live in L.A. I'm flying back tomorrow evening. I found out earlier today that I'm two months pregnant."

"Congratulations! It will be just as gorgeous as you."

"Thanks. I'll bring my daughter tomorrow so you can meet her. She's with Momma, and Reggie will come next time." Daddy and I hung out the rest of the evening.

Yolanda and I woke up early and started packing. We were going to visit Daddy again before going home. We had breakfast with Momma and went by Alexis' job. "How did it go yesterday?" She asked.

"It went well. I didn't know Daddy was a comedian."

"Oh girl, he has us rolling." She said. "When are you flying back?"

"This evening. I just wanted to stop by before we leave. How is Jaz?"

"She's fine. She flew back to New York last week to get the rest of her things."

"How is Dina?"

"Good, busy as usual. Well, I'm going to let y'all go. I have a client coming in." She hugged us. "Call me tomorrow. Have a safe flight."

Yolanda and I went to Daddy's house, and he welcomed us in. "So, this is Yolanda?" He asked.

"Yes. Say hi."

"Hi." Yolanda said, softly.

"Hi, you're a pretty girl." He said.

"Thank you."

Yolanda soon warmed up to Daddy and we all were laughing and talking. "What part of Los Angeles do y'all live in?"

"We're in Malibu."

"Oh, y'all are balling." He joked.

"You should visit sometime."

"That would be nice. I'm happy that I have another gorgeous daughter to add to my collection of gorgeous girls."

I smiled and hugged him. "Thank you."

"I'm also glad to have a gorgeous granddaughter and a future gorgeous grandchild." He said. "Now, y'all better get going before you miss your flight."

"Thank you again, Daddy."

"You're welcome."

I wrote my phone number down and gave it to him, and had Yolanda take a picture of us from my cell phone. "Call us sometime. I love you."

"I love you too. Have a safe flight and tell my son-in-law hello."

"I will. Bye." Yolanda hugged him, I took a picture of them together, and we left.

Yolanda and I landed in Los Angeles and went home. We went inside and Yolanda spoke to Reggie. He sent her upstairs to unpack, and I gave Reggie a long hug. "Are you okay?" He asked.

"Yeah." I was smiling and crying at the same time. "We laughed and talked for hours."

"I'm glad you met him, baby." He said.

"Me too. I also have something else to tell you."

"What's up?"

"I'm pregnant."

"What?"

"I'm pregnant."

Reggie picked me up and twirled me around. "My baby is having another baby?" He asked.

"Yes, I'm two months and I'm due in January."

"I love you."

"I love you too."

Dina

Chapter 24

Jaz and I are in North Carolina getting ready to drive back to New York. The movers just loaded up the moving truck for Texas. She was happy to get this done. She hasn't heard from Carlin, but I've been monitoring the vineyard and stores, and it's not looking good. Carlin seemed to have been more focused on the dealerships instead. I'm keeping this secret to keep Jaz calm, but this will be good for her. I'm getting her the vineyard back. It is beginning to suffer, and I feel it was maliciously done to break Jaz down. The only good thing Carlin has been doing was paying her alimony on time. The movers left and Jaz and I stopped for a bite to eat before driving back to New York.

Jaz and I are back on the road, and she's officially moving back to Texas tomorrow. I enjoyed her company and will miss her. She had her Benz transported to Texas and shipped the rest of her things. I was proud of Jaz. She was focused on healing, but I know she still has feelings for Kel. "So, what are your plans when you move back to Texas?"

"I'm going to focus on my son and healing." She said. "I need go on a trip but, I'm going to hang out with Daddy and save my money. Kel suggested that I rent if I decide to move out."

"That will be a good idea. It would only be temporary."

"Kel and I are going to remain friends. I want to clear my head and figure out the next move. All I want from the divorce is the vineyard and half of the money we made together."

"I got you, sis."

"Enough about me, what about you and Andrew?" She asked, changing the subject.

"I'm going to maintain a friendship with him. I talked to Daddy and of course he was against he and I dating. But I agreed with him. His wife probably can't stand me. Her aunt, who is her attorney, would do her best to come after me if Andrew and I were dating. I've worked too hard to get where I am."

"I don't blame you. Andrew is nice and seems really into you. Have you talked to Alexis?"

"Not really. I know she would disagree. But I do like Andrew."

"There is nothing wrong with that." She said. "He is very charming, but I know how he's feeling. He's vulnerable."

Getting advice from Jaz was rare. We're always giving her advice, but she has some wisdom in her. She was right. I need to slow my role with Andrew. Joan Allen is determined to come for me.

Jaz and I arrived back at my house and went inside. The road trip was fun, we took a lot of pictures, listened to music, laughed, talked, and did a little shopping along the way. We talked to Daddy and Alexis, and Yvette will be here in New York tomorrow. Yvette was cool and I'm looking forward to hanging out with her. Jaz and I unpacked and relaxed. She had an early morning flight to Texas and went to bed. I took a shower and relaxed in my bed. I thought about Andrew. I really liked him, and there is a strong attraction between us. I'll keep a professional relationship with him until his divorce is final.

I just arrived at home from taking Jaz to the airport. We hugged and cried. I'm going to miss my big sister. I dozed off on the sofa and the doorbell woke me up. It was Andrew. I missed him too. "Andrew, we need to talk."

"What's up, boo?" He asked.

"I really like you and I enjoy your company. But to protect each other, I think we need to maintain a business relationship. You're my client and you shouldn't give any ammo to Mia during the divorce process."

He nodded his head, thinking. "I understand."

"I'm sorry."

"Don't be." He said. "You're right and I will fall back."

"Thank you. Joan Allen and I never got along. I beat her in a case a few years ago and she's been bitter ever since. I'm positive she will come after me if she knew anything about us."

"Dina, I get it and I respect that. Mia has been watching my every move, but I've been careful. We'll resume after the divorce is final."

My doorbell rang again. "Yvette? Come on in."

"Hey Dina, how are you?" She asked.

"I'm fine. How was the flight?"

"It was cool. This is a nice brownstone."

"Thanks. This is my friend, Andrew. Andrew, this is my big sister Yvette."

"Nice to meet you." He said.

"You too." She said.

"Well, I'm going to let y'all catch up." He said. "I'll call you tomorrow."

"Okay." He left.

Yvette and I talked all night. She was so beautiful. She and Alexis were the same size and height, and I loved her bob haircut. Her makeup was flawless, and she was glowing. We planned to go shopping tomorrow and hang out. The phone rang and it was Daddy. "Hi Daddy, how are you?"

"Hey baby girl, I'm fine, how are you?"

"I'm great! Yvette is here. She flew in to hang out."

"Oh, tell her I said hello." He said. Daddy and I had small talk and I put him on speaker to talk to both me and Yvette. "I was calling to inform you on my doctor's appointment."

I became nervous. "Is everything okay?" Yvette asked.

"It didn't go well."

"What's wrong?"

"There is no blood circulation in my left leg." He said. "I'm getting my leg amputated."

Alexis

Chapter 25

We're all at Dad's house, getting ready to take him to the hospital. I was with Dad when the doctor told him about his leg, and my heart sank into my stomach. I've been trying to hold it together, but I cry when I'm alone. Yvette and Dina are both in town and Mom asked us to keep her informed. She and Dad have been getting along better but they were each moving on with their lives. Uncle Ernest is here, and he was quiet. Uncle Ernest, Dad's brother was here also. He was quiet. Reggie was here with Yvette, and Kel was here with Jaz. He was still standing by her. Jaz had just moved in with Dad.

Dad was getting dressed and the rest of us were sitting in the den waiting for him. He finally walked out on his cane and stood before us. "Before we go, I have something to say." He said. We gave him our undivided attention. "After the surgery and recovery, I will have to go to rehab. While I'm away, I want y'all to promise me something."

"Anything." Dina said.

"I want y'all to continue to develop a relationship with your mother. I know some of you may be upset with her but, move on and let it go. Life is short, take care of yourselves, and be happy. Jaz, you can stay here as long as you want. Yvette, Dina, and Reggie, y'all can stay here when you're in town if you want also. I don't know how long I'll be gone but, take care of everything for me, and take care of Ernest."

"We will, Daddy." Jaz said.

"I don't want any drama going on while I'm away." He demanded. We nodded. "Let's go." We left.

We're all at the hospital and Dad was in surgery. Dina burst into tears when they wheeled him off. Kel left to tend to MJ, and Patrick was about to leave. "I'm going to take the boys to my parents' house, baby." He said. "Keep me informed until I get back."

"Okay." We hugged and kissed, and he left.

Later, Roslyn, Dad's doctor finally walked out, and we jumped up. "How is he?" Dina asked.

"The surgery went well but, his blood pressure and sugar are high." She said. "We're getting it under control. He's in recovery now, sleeping but if you want to see him, it will have to be brief. I'll let you know when we get him in a room."

"Thanks." Later, we walked in Dad's room and there were all kinds of tubes in him.

Jaz walked to the bed and talked to him. Dina stood by the door, afraid, and in tears. I walked up to the bed and told him how proud I was of him. Dina finally walked to the bed, still in tears, begging him not to die. She was an emotional person and didn't take bad news well. Yvette had tears in her eyes and Reggie consoled her. Uncle Ernest stared at Dad with tears in his eyes, consoling Dina. We held hands and prayed over Dad.

We left the hospital and went to my house. The boys were in their rooms, playing video games and I talked to them. I told Patrick how well the surgery went, and my sisters and I sat in the family room. Jaz, Yvette, and I were neutral, but Dina was still a wreck.

I went back to the hospital to see Dad. His blood pressure and sugar level were getting back to normal and his leg was wrapped in bandages. He was asleep and I kissed him on his forehead. I talked to him and held his hand, praying for him to wake up. Tears formed my eyes as I watched him sleep. "Hey." I turned around and it was Mom. I hugged her, still in tears. "It's okay, honey."

"Mom, I can't lose Dad."

"I know, but your dad is a fighter." She said. "He will pull through this."

Mom and I talked, and I was starting to feel better. It was as if Mom had been around all our lives, and she was nurturing. After visiting for a while, I left, but Mom stayed at the hospital. I went to the salon but didn't have a lot of clients. Afterwards, Dina called wanting to meet for drinks. I met her at a restaurant, and we sat at the bar. We talked about Dad, and I told her that Mom was at the hospital. "What are your thoughts on Mom and Yvette?" She asked.

"Well, Yvette is the innocent one in that situation. So was Dad. But I like Yvette, she is *definitely* Dad's daughter. She has his witty ways but, she's cool. I can tell she's a little spoiled."

"Me to but, she is cool. I sensed a little anger from her also. I think she's upset about not having Daddy in her life."

"She has to take that up with Mom. I think Mom was wrong for what she did, and I admit that I am upset with her about it. But I'm trying to keep the peace for Dad's sake. He wanted us to continue to build a relationship with Mom so, that's what I'm going to do."

"To be honest, I'm not mad." She said. "Daddy raised us well and who knows what would have happened if Momma was around. She traveled a lot, and we probably wouldn't see Daddy much."

"You do have a point."

"I'm excited that you found Momma and that we have another sister. What do you think about Kel and Jaz?"

"I always thought they were the perfect match. Although the love they had for each other was never lost, I think they're doing the right thing by remaining friends. Jaz is still hurt about Carlin and Denise. She needs time to heal and get through this transition."

"I think they should get back together." She said. "But not now."

Dina then told me about how she and Andrew met. "Really, Dina? Did you ever think that you could be a rebound to him?"

"Alexis, I have thought about that. He is over his wife and they're divorce is almost final. But I did tell him that we should slow down until his divorce is final. He agreed."

"I'm sure Andrew is a nice guy but, I don't want you to end up hurt."

"I know but, I'll be fine." She said. "I think we'll be alright, and I will be cautious with my heart." Dina and I finished our drinks and left.

I thought Dina was moving too fast. I'm anxious to meet Andrew and see what he's about and how he is with my baby sister. I think Dina will be making a big mistake. Jaz and Kel may very well get back together but, I don't think she's ready. I was excited to have another sister but, the anger towards Mom was still there. I wasn't happy at all, and I can tell that Yvette wasn't either.

I went home and hugged my boys. I was happy to see them, and Patrick was out picking up dinner. He came back home, and I hugged him. Whenever my husband was around, my worries would go away. "I missed you all day."

"I missed you to, baby." He said, hugging me. "How is your dad?"

"He's getting better but was still asleep." I told him about Mom being there and my talk with Dina. "I don't know what to expect. I'm trying to be strong but, I feel like screaming sometimes."

"I know and I'm sorry. Jaz is back in Texas now and she's going to help you with your dad. Dina and Yvette won't mind getting on a plane either, and you have me. I'm sure Kel will step in. Baby, your dad has nothing to worry about and your uncle is going to be around too."

The thought of losing Dad was scary. I'm strong but I had my moments. Patrick was the only one who saw me break down. I didn't know what was going to happen next, and I was scared. My best friend Traci called me to check on Dad.

After talking with Traci, my phone rang again. "Hello?"

"Hi Alexis, this is Shonda." She said.

I was excited to hear from her. Shonda was my other best friend. It was always me, her, and Traci. She's also married to Traci's big brother. She called to check on Dad and we caught up. Shonda was a party planner and was well known throughout Texas. Her work was amazing, and she was starting to get business in other states. Her husband owned a performance hall downtown and several venues. They were entrepreneurs and wealthy. Shonda was Afrocentric, Traci was the party animal, and I was fashionable. I was known for having the best hairstyles and wardrobe. After talking to Shonda, I hung out with Patrick and our boys.

Jaz

Chapter 26

I'm glad to be back in Texas. I moved in Daddy's house and my Benz arrived. My cars are registered here, and I decided to continue living in his house and help him until he's able to get around on his own. MJ has been enjoying living with his dad and he hasn't mentioned Carlin. I haven't heard from him or Denise, but I've been receiving alimony.

I'm on my way to visit Daddy. He was still recovering but doing better. I walked in his hospital room, and he was watching TV, eating. "Hey." He said.

"Hi Daddy, how are you?"

"I'm alright, how are you doing?" I hugged him.

I visited with Daddy and held back my tears. Although he was in a good mood and making me laugh, seeing him like this hurt. Daddy was my hero and protector and now seemed helpless in my eyes. "How long will you be in here?"

"I don't know." He said. "Maybe another week or two and then I'm off to rehab."

"I miss you, Daddy."

"I miss you all too." I began to cry. "Jaz don't start. I'm fine."

"I know but, I hate this is happening."

"I did this to myself." He said. "Take care of yourselves so you won't end up like me. But things happen and the important thing is to remain positive about it. I'm at peace with this."

I wish I was as sanguine as he was. "I'm staying in your house until you get well."

"I appreciate that Jaz but, don't put your life on hold for me. Go out and live. You're at a new start so, enjoy life and rebuild. How is my grandson?"

"He's fine, I'm going to see him when I leave here." I then asked Daddy's advice about Kel. "When I'm around Kel, everything is better. Sometimes I have to catch myself when I see him. I want to hug and kiss him as if we are together, but we agreed to be friends. What should I do?"

"Well, I think you should follow your heart but use your brain." He said. "A lot of people ignore that because of fear. Love is never unsure, it's black and white. Humans create a grey area. If your heart is telling you to be with him, then go for it, but after your divorce is final. It's not like Kel is someone new. You've dated before and you have a son together. But, if you want to know how he feels, tell him how you feel first and wait for his reaction. Listen to what he has to say. At the same time, make sure it's love you're feeling and not loneliness. Although you're over Carlin, you're still susceptible to anything."

"That is what is confusing, Daddy. I can't tell the difference."

"Sure, you can. Any slight of doubt or if you see a red flag, it's a warning, and you'll know to fall back. I suggest you use this time to heal and get yourself together. That should be your main focus even after talking to Kel." After visiting with Daddy, I left.

I went over to Kel's house, still thinking about what Daddy told me. I was nervous but excited at the same time. I arrived at Kel's house and butterflies filled my stomach. I took a deep breath and rang the doorbell. "What's up?" He asked, opening the door. "Is that your Benz?"

He was checking it out. "Yes, I had it transported."

"It's nice! You and your dad be rolling!" We laughed.

Kel looked *so* good – casually dressed in jeans, a polo shirt, and sneakers. "How are you?"

"I'm cool, come on in."

I walked inside and noticed the aroma. "What smells so good?"

"I smoked some meat for me and MJ." He said.

"Oh, where is MJ?"

"He's in the back. I'll get him."

I stared at the same picture I stare at every time I come here. "Hi, Momma." MJ said, running towards me.

"Hey! How are you?"

"I'm fine." He sat next to me and hugged me. "Are you staying, daddy cooked?"

I looked up at Kel and he shrugged his shoulders. "Well, is there enough food for me?"

"Of course." He said.

MJ got excited. I stayed in the living room and talked with MJ. The food was ready, and we ate together in the dining room. Kel smoked ribs, brisket, he made baked beans, homemade macaroni and cheese, greens, and potato salad. It was so good and fulfilling. Kel can cook anything, and he can bake. He baked a homemade chocolate cake, and it melted in my mouth. "Kel, this was good. You still got it."

He laughed. "Thanks, this is all I do." He said. MJ finished eating and went to his room. Kel grabbed a beer and we moved to the living room. "So, how are you?"

"I'm okay. I'm glad to be back in Texas. I decided to stay in my dad's house until he's able to get around. I came here straight from the hospital."

"How is he?"

"He's getting better and in good spirits. He was making me laugh and I was trying to hold back the tears but, they began to flow. Seeing him like that is hard."

"I know this is easier said than done but, you have to be strong." He said.

"I know but, it's hard. Other than that, I've been focusing on rebuilding myself. This legal separation seems to be moving slow but, I got it started."

He nodded and smiled. "I'm proud of you, Jaz."

"Thank you. Thank you for being there for me. I wouldn't have gotten through all of this without you, Kel."

"You know I'm here for you, no matter what. Your dad is like a father to me too. If your dad doesn't want his truck anymore, I got dibs."

I laughed. "It's still in good condition. Everyone wants that truck." I took a deep breath and listened to my heart. "Kel, I have something that I need to get off my chest."

"What's up?" He asked.

"I'm falling in love with you again. I always loved you and I think about you all the time." I started to get emotional and everything I held in came out. "I don't want you to think that you're a rebound because you're not. But I would like for us to be together again."

He pulled me close to him and looked me in my eyes. "Jaz, I love you too." He said. "I always have, and I think about you all the time too. I know I wouldn't be a rebound guy, but I don't think you're ready."

My heart stopped. "How would you know?"

"You're vulnerable right now. You just left your husband, and your dad is in the hospital. I do care about you, and I want my shoulder to be the one you cry on. I have to be sure that I'm ready to do this again too."

I sat there and forced myself to understand his feelings. "Okay Kel, I don't want to rush you. I am working on a lot of things with myself – healing and rebuilding. But I'd like for you to think about it."

"I will."

"I should get going. I'm mentally drained." I stood. "Thanks for dinner, it was amazing."

He stood there, staring at me. "Anytime." I said bye to MJ and left.

I drove back to Daddy's house in tears. I wish there was something I could do to convince Kel to be with me but, you can't rush love. I hope I'm not in this alone and I wish he wouldn't have kissed me a while back. This better not be a game. I walked in the house and stretched out on the sofa, still thinking about Kel. The phone rang and startled me. "Hello?"

"Hey Jaz." Alexis said. "Where are you?"

"I'm at Daddy's house. What's up?"

"I'm at the hospital. Something happened with Dad."

"What's going on?"

"He had a stroke." I dropped the phone and froze. I began to shake. I was just talking to Daddy, and he was fine. "Jaz, are you there?"

I picked up the phone and cried. "I'm on my way."

I rushed to the hospital and found Alexis. She was holding it together, but her eyes were red. "I haven't heard anything yet." She said. "It doesn't look good."

"Have you talked to Dina, Yvette, or Uncle Ernest?"

"They are flying in tonight and Uncle Ernest is on his way. Mom is on her way too."

"I was just here earlier."

"I was here this morning." She said. "Roslyn called me, and I hurried here."

Roslyn walked out. "How is he?"

She shook her head. "It's not good." She said. "He's in a coma."

Yvette

Chapter 27

It's been two weeks since I've gone to Texas. Daddy was still in a coma, and we've been hoping and praying that he will get better. I would give anything to hear another joke from him. This is what makes me more upset with Momma. I missed out on everything with Daddy. But I can only imagine how my sisters feel. They missed out on everything with Momma. Jaz was glad to be back in Texas and decided to stay in Daddy's house. Dina was busy as usual, and we planned to hang out again soon. I find out the gender of the baby next month and we're hoping it's a boy. Reggie is excited and Yolanda was looking forward to becoming a big sister. I hope Daddy hangs in there to see his new grandchild. I haven't talked to Momma much. She's been working and checking on Daddy.

Reggie and I started the process on opening a new office in Las Vegas. I've been resting from all the excitement with Daddy, and Reggie's been traveling back and forth from here to Vegas. I can't wait until we're done. We thought about buying a house there as well. This was our only home, but I loved Vegas.

I sat on the lanai and watched Reggie and Yolanda play in the pool. I began to imagine them as me and Daddy again. The phone rang and it was Momma. "Hello?"

"Hey."

"Hi Momma. You're in California?"

"Yeah but, I have something to tell you." She said, sounding down.

I became nervous. "What's wrong?"

"Alexis just called me and said that Morris' organs were shutting down. He woke up out of his coma last night, had another stroke, and went into a coma again." My heart started racing and Reggie saw the fear in my face. "We need to be at the hospital tomorrow afternoon. I'm flying to Texas tonight."

"Okay, I'm going to call Alexis now."

"Call me when you get there." She said. "I love you."

"I love you too."

Reggie walked over to me. "Is everything okay?" He asked. I explained to him what happened and cried. He walked me to our bedroom and wrapped his arms around me. "It's going be okay, baby. Lay here and relax while I take care of Yolanda. I'll be back."

I laid there and called Alexis. "Hello?" She answered.

"Hey, it's Yvette."

"Hey sis." She heard me crying. "Yvette, don't worry yourself, okay? Jaz and I are about to go back to the hospital but, everyone needs to be here tomorrow."

"Okay, we'll be there."

"I love you and call me when y'all get here."

"I love you too."

"If anything changes, I'll call you."

We hung up and I cried harder. I can't believe how strong she is. I then called Momma back. "Hello?" She answered.

"I just got off the phone with Alexis. She and Jaz were on their way to the hospital. Have you talked to Dina or Jaz?"

"I haven't talked to Jaz. I talked to Dina, and she was taking it hard."

"I'll call her, and I'll see you tomorrow."

"Okay, I'm heading to the jet now."

We hung up and I called Dina. "Hello?" She answered, crying.

When I heard her, I cried again. "It's Yvette, are you okay?"

"No, I'm not." She said, sobbing. "I'm flying down in the morning."

"We are too. Is someone staying there with you?"

"Andrew is on his way." She said. "He's spending the night."

"Okay, I'll see you tomorrow. I love you."

"I love you too."

Later Reggie came back in the room, and I told him what was going on. He had the jet gassed up for tomorrow, and we started packing. I lied in the bed, with my mind going in different directions. I pulled myself together and went upstairs to talk to Yolanda. I told her what was going on and she hugged me. We ate dinner together and I was starting to feel better but, I was still thinking about Daddy. Lisa called to check on me, I had told her about me finding Daddy and my sisters. She was aware of his illness and offered to assist if needed. After dinner, Reggie and Yolanda cleaned the kitchen for me, and I relaxed in the family room. Momma, Alexis, and Jaz all sent me text messages, keeping me updated on Daddy. He wasn't doing well. Yolanda went upstairs and I sat in a daze. Reggie wrapped his arms around me, and I fell asleep.

Dina

Chapter 28

I'm at home, packing for tomorrow morning. I've been crying all evening and my eyes were red and puffy. Momma, Alexis, and Jaz were all at the hospital with Daddy, and sent me text messages keeping me updated. I washed my face and calmed myself down. I sat my bags in the living room and waited for Andrew. Yvette sounded so crushed when I talked to her earlier and I hope she's okay, carrying a baby. I sat there and started crying again, then the doorbell rang. I opened the door and Andrew instantly grabbed me and hugged me. I cried again. "Come on, let's sit down." He said.

I couldn't stop crying and he held me in his arms. "I'm flying to Texas in the morning. Alexis told me that we all need to be at the hospital. I don't know what's going to happen."

"Just think positive and do what your dad would have wanted you to do."

"I can't." I cried again.

"Dina, you can." He said. "That's what your dad would want, judging by what you say about him."

I began to pull myself together, thinking about what he said. Daddy wanted us to be strong with whatever may happen. Andrew kept me company and I received phone calls and text messages from people I haven't heard from in a long time – relatives, classmates, and friends back home. My phone rang and I didn't recognize the number. The call was from Atlanta. "Hello?"

"Hi, is this Dina?" A woman asked.

"Yes, who's calling?"

"Hey Dina, it's Donna!"

I was happy to hear from her. Donna and I went to high school together and she went to college in Atlanta. We haven't talked since her wedding. I'm tall, she was only five-foot-two, and high yellow like me. She and I were close friends. "How have you been?"

"I've been doing well." She said. "My sister Traci told me about your dad. I'm so sorry about what happened."

"Thank you so much Donna. It's tough and we don't know what's going to happen. I'm flying to Texas in the morning. It doesn't look good."

"Dina, keep praying and try to be strong. I know how close you are to Mr. Morris. He was like another dad to me. I remember the fun slumber parties we used to have." I laughed.

Donna and I always had sleepovers and studied together. We were nerds but knew how to have fun. Her parents were cool also and the ladies had crushes on her two brothers. Her big sister was gorgeous, and she and Alexis are friends. Donna's husband was a cardiologist, and she was an OB/GYN in Atlanta. She had her own practice and was doing well. I was happy for her, and we both were striving to be successful. She wanted to deliver babies and I wanted to be a lawyer. We caught up reminiscing on the good old days and it was the distraction I needed. We agreed to stay in touch.

It's five-thirty in the morning and I was having an Uber pick me up at six-thirty to take me to the airport. "Good morning, sleepy head." Andrew said.

"Good morning." I sat up and felt exhausted.

"Walk me to the door." He said.

"Thanks for staying with me."

"You didn't need to be alone."

"I'm going to get dressed and head out."

"Alright, call me when you get there and be strong, baby." He said, pulling me close to him.

"I will." We kissed and hugged each other tight. "Bye."

Everyone is at the hospital, including Uncle Ernest. The kids weren't here. We've been waiting on Roslyn to come out for an hour, and I was getting impatient. Andrew and I have been sending each other text messages. Roslyn finally walked out. "Morris is on life support." She said. My heart dropped. "There's nothing we can do. His body has shut down and the longer he's on the machine, the longer he will suffer." Alexis held her head down, and Yvette and I began crying. Jaz was in a daze and Momma was in shock. Uncle Ernest stood there, speechless. "I'm so sorry. A decision needs to be made." She walked off.

"Let's go to my house." Momma said.

We're all sitting in Momma's massive family room, quiet. We were all in tears and comforting each other. I couldn't hold it together and wanted Andrew here with me. "What are we going to do?" I had to break the silence and that's all I could think about.

"What can we do?" Jaz asked.

"Look, Dad isn't going to make it so, we might as well take him off life support." Alexis said. "He has suffered enough."

"Fine, I'm going upstairs to lay down." Yvette said getting up, and Reggie followed her.

"I'm leaving." Jaz said. "You ready, Dina?"

"Yeah."

"We'll see y'all in the morning." Alexis said.

Jaz and I went back to Daddy's house. Later that evening, I called Andrew and told him what was going on. He insisted on flying down tonight. Alexis then called letting us know that she and Yvette were on their way.

They arrived and we sat in the den. "What time are we doing this tomorrow?" Alexis asked.

"Can we do it at noon?" Jaz asked.

"It doesn't matter." Yvette said.

"Okay, I'll call Traci's cousin. He's a minister and I'll ask him to meet us there at eleven." Alexis said. "We'll take him off at noon. But there is one thing that I was wondering about – the will."

"I have it." They looked at me. "I have the will."

"When were you going to tell us?" Jaz asked.

"Daddy didn't want me to tell y'all. I'll read it after the funeral. He changed a few things in it."

"Okay, let's not get upset." Alexis said. "We'll just wait until then. I'll talk to Uncle Ernest."

We reminisced on the good times with Daddy. Yvette sat back and listened and now, it's time for Momma to step in. We talked to Uncle Ernest, and he was being strong, but we saw the pain in his eyes. It was just him and Daddy. Soon, I left to pick up Andrew from the airport and we went back to Daddy's house. Although we're maintaining a friendship, I was glad he was here.

It's almost noon and we're all at the hospital waiting on Roslyn. She finally came out and I was nervous. "Okay, you may come in." She said. We followed her to his room, and the minister, *Brother Parks*, who is also Donna's cousin, stood beside his bed with the bible in his hand. We said our goodbye's one at a time and we were all in tears but, Alexis took it the hardest. Uncle Ernest was being strong.

Momma walked to the bed in tears. "Well Morris, we've had our ups and downs." She said. "But we've had more downs. Out of it all, we had four beautiful girls. We all reunited, and you and I talked after arguing. You did a good job raising Dina, Jaz, and Alexis. I know you will watch over us and you will always be in my heart. We had some good times together and now, it's time to go home where there will be no more suffering. I love you and I'll see you when I get there. Goodbye." Momma walked away from his bed and the minister said a prayer.

The minister left the room to give us time alone with Daddy. Yvette stayed outside the room and Patrick walked Alexis out. Jaz decided at the last minute that she didn't want to be in the room and Kel walked her out. Momma and

I were still in the room and Andrew held me. The machine was turned off and we watched him take his last breath. Momma and I broke down, and Andrew walked me out. I nearly screamed and now, I wished I would have walked out. Andrew sat me down and Alexis was hugging me. We went back to Momma's house.

Alexis

Chapter 29

It has been nearly two weeks since Dad passed and today will be my first time going to his house. Today is the funeral and Patrick and my boys were dressed, waiting on me. The wake yesterday was very emotional, and Dad looked peaceful, but I remained strong. I don't know how today will go. Dina has been in town the entire time and is staying at Dad's house with Jaz. Yvette and her family were at Mom's house. Since Dad passed away, my sisters and I have gotten closer. We would check on each other, hang out at Mom's house, and they would come over. I wasn't ready to go to Dad's house knowing he was no longer there. Yvette helped Jaz and Dina clean his house, but I refused to go. We have discussed renovating it but at a later time. I've checked on Uncle Ernest, and he was crushed. It was just him and Dad, and now he's alone. They were close.

I wore my black jumpsuit, designer belt, and pearls. My hair was up, I applied my makeup, and carried my designer shoulder bag. I grabbed my sunglasses and we headed to Dad's house. I became nervous when we parked in the driveway and was taking deep breaths. We went inside and tears filled my eyes. I looked over at Dad's recliner chair where he always sat and cried. Mom and my sisters hugged me. Dina was sitting to herself, and her friend Andrew was with her. I checked on her and she was in a daze. She still looked beautiful in her black pantsuit. People were checking on her and was excited to see her. She was rarely seen, and people flock to her when she's around. Yvette met a few family members, and they were elated to know about her. Jaz was talking to family and Kel was still by her side. I needed some fresh air and walked outside, concealing my emotions, trying to remain strong. "Are you alright, baby girl?" Uncle Ernest asked.

"I'm fine. I'm just nervous and ready to get this over with."

He hugged me. "Me too. I'm going inside. Where is Victoria?"

"She's in the den."

Uncle Ernest went in the house, and Dina walked outside. "Where are the limos?" Dina asked.

I looked down the street and saw them. "There they go."

"Alexis, I'm so nervous."

"Me too."

Everyone walked outside and formed a circle. The minister, the preacher prayed, and we got in the limos. We arrived at the church and lined up outside. When Dina saw the hearse, tears rolled down her face. Jaz, Yvette, and I were still holding it together. After we lined up, the funeral directors opened the doors, and we walked inside while the congregation stood, singing. My heart was racing, and tears flowed when I saw Dad's casket. We sat on the front pew, Uncle Ernest sat next to Dina, and Mom sat with our kids behind us. Kel sat with the pallbearers and Andrew sat towards the back.

The minister started the eulogy, and the choir sang. A few friends of the family, including Roslyn, gave their remarks about Dad. Then Uncle Ernest spoke. "Hello everyone." He said. "I'm Morris' brother, Ernest, and I want everyone to know how much fun my big brother was. We all know that Morris was a big joker and loved the blues but, he was a father figure to everyone. He and I were close, and he taught me a lot. He was a very responsible person and adored his daughters. They always came first and fathers like that are rare to find. Morris and I haven't seen or spoken to each other since our parents died because, I thought life was a joke. We disagreed on a lot of things that caused us not to speak. I'm glad that he and I rekindled our relationship. I couldn't handle not having our parents around and I got myself into trouble but, when I heard that my brother was in the hospital, I had to see him. I went up there and he and I talked for a long time. He was discharged from the hospital, and we hung out again. Then, he went back in the hospital. He went into a coma, and I went to see him when he woke up. He told me he discovered that he had another daughter. I was excited to have another niece. We began cracking jokes, and he asked if I was ever going to get married, and I told him *no*." Everyone laughed aware of his character. Uncle Ernest was a bachelor and charmed women. He was still dapper for his age and people loved him. "We caught up and apologized to each other for what happened in the past, then out of the blue, he told me that he was tired and ready to go home. I told him that I wanted him to go home to so we can have another card party. He said he wasn't talking about the house. He was ready to go *home* and told me to leave. I hugged him and told him that I loved him. When I walked out of his room, he had a stroke and the doctors rushed in. He went into another coma, and I cried my eyes out when I got home. To my nieces and Victoria, I love you and I'm here for you."

Mom then spoke. "I want everyone to know that Morris was a great father to our girls." She said. "Morris, Ernest, and I used to hang out and party all the time. Morris was a big joker, loved the blues, and was good at dominos. No one could beat him. He was a very good person, and we had our differences and went our separate ways but, we were a well-known couple back in those days. Morris was also a *very* dominate person and a fighter. If anyone heard about a fight that broke out, you knew he was involved, somehow. But now it's time for him to hang up the gloves and go home. To my daughters and Ernest, I love you and I'm here for you." Mom sat down and Dina went to say a few words.

When Dina started talking, she began to cry. Nearly everyone was in tears, watching her breakdown. Andrew walked her to her seat and sat with her. The rest of us were too choked up to talk. The preacher then said a few words and the choir stood and sang. The funeral home directors opened Dad's casket and I lost it. The choir continued singing as everyone viewed Dad's body and exited the church. Roslyn, Dina's best friend Donna, my best friend Traci, and other close friends hugged each of us and walked out. Kel sat with Jaz, and Andrew stayed with Dina. Reggie walked Yvette to the casket, and she kissed him. She cried and Reggie walked her outside. We all broke down, Dina yelled for Dad to wake up, and Mom comforted Uncle Ernest. Everyone stood outside, hugging, and talking to us. The pallbearers carried Dad's casket to the hearse and Dina broke down again. Everyone consoled Dina, and Andrew and her friend Donna walked her to the limo.

Everyone was at the cemetery and after the preacher dismissed us, we each took a rose from Dad's casket. We sat in silence watching the undertakers lower the casket into the ground. I had stopped crying but was in a daze, staring at the casket. Jaz and Yvette sat in silence as tears rolled down their faces. Dina was still in tears, sobbing, trying to be strong but couldn't. As Andrew walked her to the limo, family members and friends were hugging her. The rest of us finally stood, and everyone consoled us as we made our way to the limos. Patrick had me wrapped in his arms. Everyone went back to the church for dinner and Dina eventually stopped crying but was quiet. We planned to meet at Dad's house to discuss the will.

It has been a week since Dad's funeral, and I was mentally and emotionally drained. I still thought about Dad and had gone back to his house, checking on my sisters. I went back to work at the salon yesterday but only booked a few clients. I wasn't in the mood but needed a distraction. After I finished my last client, I went home. Patrick and the boys were gone, and I relaxed in the family room. Soon, the doorbell rang. "Hi Mom, come on in."

She hugged me and it was what I needed. "How are you, honey?" She asked.

"I'm okay." She joined me in the family room. "I went back to work but didn't book a lot of clients."

"I understand. Where is my son-in-law and grandsons?"

"I don't know. I just got home, and they were gone. How have you been?"

"I've been okay. I'm about to start traveling again. I wanted to check on y'all."

"I think I'm going to take more time off."

"You should." She agreed. "Why not open your own salon, Alexis? You can set your own hours and do your own thing."

"I've thought about it but, I don't know if I would have the time."

"Sure, you would. You're a boss."

Mom was right. I was told that I should run my own hair salon and I knew the finances would be better. My clientele was strong, and I know they would follow me. "I'm going to talk to Patrick. I know he will agree. He's been supporting this idea."

Mom smiled and stood. "Well, when you're ready, I will buy you one."

I paused. "Buy me one?"

"Yes. Alexis you are so talented, and you've done a lot for your sisters and your dad. Let me buy you a salon. I insist." She said. "I'm going to buy you and Patrick a house too. I'm going to be more involved in your lives and although y'all are grown, I'm still going to take care of you. I won't take no for an answer. I'll be in touch. I love you."

She hugged me. "I love you too." I walked her to the door.

"I'll see you when I get back." She left.

I sat on the sofa thinking about her offer. I felt guilty accepting it because a part of me was still upset with her for not being in our lives. But I want my own salon and Patrick and I have talked about moving. "Hey." Patrick said walking through the door.

"Hey, where are the boys?"

He hugged and kissed me. "They're with Kel and Jaz hanging out with MJ. I thought we could go out and enjoy the evening with my brother and Traci."

I smiled. "Okay, where are we going?"

"Traci's restaurant. Harold and Shonda will be there too." I was getting excited. "Get dressed."

Patrick and I got dressed. This is what I needed. He always looked after me. I told him about Mom wanting to buy us a house and me a salon. He agreed that we should let her as long as I was okay with it. It was the middle of summer, and the Texas heat was suffocating. I wore my cropped jeans, a tank top, and sandals. I put on my jewelry, applied my makeup, and wore my hair back in a ponytail. Patrick looked nice in his denim shorts, a designer t-shirt, and sneakers. He had a new haircut and smelled good. We kissed, I took a picture of us, and posted it on my social media page.

We arrived at Traci's restaurant, and it was crowded. She had a table for us, and we walked across the bridge into the restaurant. Traci's restaurant was on the lake and the view was amazing. The deejay was playing eighties and nineties music and the vibe was nice. They were already seated we had the perfect view. We greeted each other and ordered drinks. I looked around and everyone was dancing in their seats to the music, singing. People were out on the lake in their boats and jet skis. Shonda, Traci, and I were taking pictures together and we ordered our meals and talked. Traci had the best bartenders and served seafood, Italian, and southern cuisines. It was amazing. The sun began to set and gave a beautiful golden glow. I missed Dad and I know he's no longer suffering. I'm going to hold on to his promise and give Mom a chance. But I still had questions for her.

Jaz

Chapter 30

It's been a month since Daddy's funeral. The service was nice and there were a lot of people who attended. I'm still dealing with his passing and holding on to his words of wisdom. In the will, he left us the house and an equal share of his retirement. We decided to keep Daddy's house and renovate it. It needed work. We planned to host holidays there, and Dina and Yvette would be staying in the house when they're in town. Alexis donated Daddy's clothes and we plan to donate his furniture when we start the renovations. He left his truck to Uncle Ernest and his new Cadillac to us. We keep it at his house for Yvette and Dina to drive when they're in town. We gave Momma photos of us growing up, and Yvette photos of Daddy. He left each of us a letter and told me to take care of MJ, and to follow my heart. He also wrote that he loved all of us and told Momma that he was with her. He told us to take care of her and stay close to one another, including Uncle Ernest. I used my share of Daddy's money to open a brokerage account for MJ. I'm going to teach him how to buy and trade stock. I haven't heard from Carlin or Denise, and I'm sure someone told them about Daddy's passing. I received phone calls from my high school and college friends. One of my friends, Juanita, had been in touch. I haven't seen or heard from her in a long time prior to the funeral. I can't wait for the three of us to hang out again. It was me, Tonya, and Nita. Nita's husband and Kel were good friends too.

I've been focusing on starting over and was glad that my legal separation was almost over. This has been a long year and I'm filing for my divorce in January. I've been brainstorming on ideas for my vineyard and stores. I don't know how business is going now that Carlin is running them. I'm going to fight for them and move the business here in Texas. I decided to move out of Daddy's house after we buried him. I couldn't handle being in the house. I rented a house just outside Momma's neighborhood. It was a small craftsman house with a big, covered porch and patio, a car port, and a detached garage toward the back of the house. I've been here a week and was settled in, and I bought MJ new bedroom furniture. He and Kel loved the house, but MJ was still staying with his dad.

I just finished the laundry and as I was walking to my bedroom, my phone rang. "Hello?"

"Hey, it's Yvette." She said.

"Hey girl! What's up?" It was good to hear her voice. "How is the baby?"

"The baby is fine." She said. "I was calling to invite you to our Labor Day barbecue here in Malibu. Everyone else is coming."

"You know I don't miss any parties. I will be there."

"Good. Bring MJ and Kel. There will be plenty of food and there is plenty of room for y'all to stay here."

"Okay, I'll see you then." I then called Alexis.

We had small talk, and it was good to hear my big sister's voice. We've all been busy with our own families and getting back to our lives since the funeral. "Mom is buying us a house north of here, and we move in November." She said.

"I can't wait to see it."

"The house was already under construction, and they are closing out the community. Yvette put our house on the market and so far, we've had one person look at it. But we got a lot of views on the internet. How are you and Kel?"

"We're still the same."

"Take your time. We will see you in Malibu."

I then called Dina. "Hey Dina!"

"What's up, Jaz?" She asked.

"What's been going on?"

"Work, work, work. How are you and Kel?"

"Still the same."

"How is my nephew?" She asked.

"He's fine, he's with his dad now."

"We are going to Yvette's for Labor Day."

"*We*? Is Andrew going?"

"Yes, he is." She said. "He's been so good to me. We're spending the day together and he's on his way. But we will see you in Malibu."

"Take care!" We hung up and I finished my laundry.

I took a shower and washed my hair. I left it in an afro and put on a maxi dress. I sat on my patio and the winds had picked up. It was dark and cloudy, and I saw flashes of lightening. Although it was windy, it felt nice. I thought about Kel. I want to be with him *so* bad but, I'm still legally married.

I went back inside, and the doorbell rang. "Kel? What are you doing here? Where is MJ?"

"He's with my mom." He said.

Damn, he looked good. "Come on in."

He walked in and I was checking him out. He was casually dressed in jeans, a t-shirt, sneakers, and a ball cap. He smelled good too. We sat in the living room. "How have you been?"

"I've been good."

"I'm talking about since the funeral." He said.

"I'm better. I still think about him a lot but, I'm okay. Thanks for asking." He sat there like he had something on his mind. "What's up?"

"How is the legal separation going?" He sat back on the sofa. "I think about you all the time and I've been giving us a lot of thought."

"Me too. I can file for my divorce in January. I'm patiently waiting. I don't know what he's doing, and I haven't heard from him or Denise."

"I just want things to be right between us and I think we can make this work."

My heart wanted to explode. "Really?"

"Yes." He said. "I love you Jaz and I'm not letting you go like I did before. Since you're still married, let's stay friends, respect the boundaries, and move forward when you're divorced."

"Okay." We shared a long passionate kiss and spent the day together. It began to storm, he ordered pizza, and we watched movies we saw back when we were dating. We listened to music as we looked through my old CD collection and had a few drinks. I looked at the clock and it was eleven. "Oh, look at the time. How long is your mom keeping MJ?"

"He's spending the night."

"Okay, you can help me in the kitchen."

We cleaned our mess, and he grabbed me and kissed me. We were all over each other and I stopped him. "We better stop." I can't wait to be divorced.

Chapter 31

I've gone to Texas once since Daddy's funeral to help my sisters clean his house and to visit Momma. I used my share of his money to start a college fund for our unborn baby. Daddy's message to me in his letter was to take care of my family and he was glad that we met. I still think about him to this day, and I wish he could be here to visit us in Malibu and spend time with my family. But I know he's here in spirit. The funeral was beautiful, and Daddy looked like he was asleep. He looked so peaceful, but I was torn. I spent a lot of time with him before he passed and was glad that we met. I was still bitter about not having him in my life all these years, and not being around my sisters. I was willing to move forward and focus on building my relationship with my sisters.

Yolanda and I are at my friend Lisa's house. She was hanging out with her daughter while Lisa and I were talking on her lanai. She and her family flew to Texas for Daddy's funeral. We didn't expect to see them and were grateful for their support. "How are you getting along with your sisters?" She asked.

"We get along well. They will be in town tomorrow for our Labor Day barbecue. I wish you and your family could attend."

"My in-laws are having a barbecue and we already told them we would be there. I would have loved to meet the rest of your family."

"You will one day. They're pretty cool."

"How are you getting along with Miss. Victoria?" She asked.

I sighed. "We get along but, it's clear that we're avoiding the elephant in the room."

"What's that?"

"Her not allowing me to have a relationship with my dad. All I keep thinking about is, what if she never found him? Would she had reached out to him without me going to her, to tell him about me?"

"I understand you're upset, and you have every right to be." She said.

"I wish I would have known him longer. I've never met my grandparents. They died before I was born."

"Well, when the time is right, talk to your mom. You clearly have a lot on your mind and anger built up inside."

"I do Lisa. I'm trying to be peaceful and honor my dad's wish but, I can't get over it."

Its Labor Day weekend and we have a full house. There were people inside playing pool, outside in the swimming pool, and on the balcony. Reggie, Patrick, and Kel had to barbecue more meat because more people came than we expected. Dina and Andrew were in the pool and the teenagers were teaching Jaz new dances. I was glad she and Kel were rekindling their relationship. Momma was in the kitchen preparing more food and I was walking around. We hired a deejay, and he played eighties hip hop, and if I wasn't pregnant, I would be dancing.

After the party, we cleaned the house. Later, the guys and the kids fell asleep, and the ladies sat in the family room and talked. "Yvette, I love this house." Dina said.

"Thanks."

"When will your house be ready, Alexis?" Dina asked.

"In November." She said. "I can't wait. How are you and Andrew?"

"We're fine." Dina said. "We're still friends, but he's been very patient and his final court date for his divorce is the day before Momma's birthday." She looked at Momma.

She smiled. "Well, y'all know I'm having a big party in Newport Beach so, come on out." She said. "It's going to be family and close friends."

"We'll be there."

"So, Yvette, are you having a boy or a girl?" Jaz asked.

"I'm having a boy." They congratulated me. "Reggie and I are done having children. How are you and Kel?"

"We are better than before." She said, smiling. "We're still friends though."

"Good!" Dina said. "Jaz and Kel were the hottest couple back in the day. There were a lot of jealous men and women. When y'all get back together, there are going to be some broken hearts."

"Oh well. Life goes on."

"How did y'all like the barbecue?"

"It was fun." Dina said. "Reggie, Patrick, and Kel can cook too."

"Yes, they can barbecue for my party." Momma suggested. "You know girls, during the party earlier, I was thinking about your dad. It brought back memories from when your dad and I used to have house parties and listen to blues music. I can see that it was passed down to y'all."

"Jaz had those kinds of parties, until she got with Carlin." Alexis said.

"Why did you have to go there?" Jaz asked.

"It's true. Jaz, before you and Carlin met, you and Kel had the biggest parties, and the entire neighborhood was there. You had block parties and everything."

"We plan to have more parties too."

"Well girls, I'm going to bed." Momma said, standing up. "I'm driving back to Newport Beach tomorrow. Goodnight."

"Goodnight."

"I'm going to bed too." Jaz said. "We're flying back early in the morning. Goodnight."

"We're leaving tomorrow night but, I'm going to bed myself." Alexis said. "I want to go to sleep before Patrick starts snoring. Goodnight girls."

"Goodnight."

"Yvette, I had fun." Dina said. "We all needed this since Daddy's funeral."

"Yes, we did. You know Dina, I think about Daddy every day. I wish he was here."

"Me too. I can still feel his presence around us, and I know he's not suffering. Daddy suffered for a very long time and I'm sure he's happy where he is."

"You're right. Well, when are you and Andrew leaving?"

"We're flying back tomorrow evening." She said. "I'll be busy getting ready for his final court date. But you can still visit since we never got a chance to hang out."

"Sounds like a plan." I turned out the lights and went to bed.

The party was fun, and I was glad that everyone came. I lied in bed in Reggie's arms, thinking about everything. I missed Daddy but was glad I met him. I still had questions for Momma but, my focus was my unborn child, my husband, and Yolanda.

Dina

Chapter 32

It's Friday morning and Andrew and I are in the courtroom, waiting for the judge. Andrew was nervous and didn't know what to expect. Mia and Joan were sitting on the other side with their noses in the air.

Soon, the judge walked out, and we stood. We reviewed the deposition and Joan began. "Your honor, since the deposition, my client has found employment but would still like to have the house and cars." Joan said.

"Why does she need all the cars?" The judge asked.

I didn't understand that. "She's having problems with the vehicle she has now, and her credit isn't good enough to purchase another one."

"Do you have proof of her income?"

"Yes ma'am." Joan handed the bailiff Mia's proof of income from her new job. "That's all she's bringing home."

The judge looked at the papers but said nothing. "Mrs. Hicks, why do you want the house?"

"I need a place to stay." Mia said, sounding innocent. "The lease on the condo will expire in three months."

"Well, with your income, you can't afford the mortgage."

"Your honor, that house means something to me, and I don't want to lose it."

"I understand but, I'm sure Mr. Hicks doesn't want to risk you taking over the mortgage."

"Your honor, my client also wants spousal support." Joan stated, changing the subject.

"Why?"

"Because with her income, she can't afford a decent way of living."

"I see." The judge then turned to me. "Miss. James?"

"Your honor, my client wishes to keep the house and his vehicles. With his income, he can make the payments on both the house and cars."

"May I see his proof of income?"

"Yes ma'am." I handed the papers to the bailiff, and she looked at them. "Okay, why should I grant you the house, Mr. Hicks?"

"Your honor, Mia just wants the house to ruin my credit." Andrew said.

"That's not true!" Mia shouted.

The judge banged her gavel. "Mrs. Hicks, you had your chance to talk!" She yelled.

"Your honor, Mrs. Hicks hasn't been able to keep up with payments on anything and they're bank account balance has dropped tremendously due to a massive number of purchases." I handed their bank statement to the bailiff.

The judge looked at them and looked at Mia. "It's showing that you have done a lot of shopping, Mrs. Hicks." The judge said. "You've spent thirty-thousand dollars within a few months, and with your new income, you should have been able to make ends meet." Joan rolled her eyes at me, and Mia gave Andrew an evil look. The judge looked at the papers and back at Mia. "Mrs. Hicks, can you explain this because, you haven't said anything."

"Yes, your honor." She said. "I needed shoes, clothes, and my car needed repairs."

"All of your clothes, shoes, and car repairs totaled up to thirty-thousand dollars?"

"Yes, your honor." Mia said, sticking to her story.

"Mrs. Hicks, you have a serious spending problem." The judge said. "I'm looking at the stores you purchased everything from, and you can't afford to spend money like this. This is ridiculous!"

"Your honor, my client also wants Andrew to buy her out if she doesn't get the house." Joan said.

"I know, because she wants to shop!" The judge yelled.

"Your honor, I need a place to stay and a new car." Mia said, starting to cry. "I don't think it's fair that he gets to live better than me."

"Mrs. Hicks, you need to be more responsible and cautious about your purchases. Your priorities aren't straight. You stand here, and practically lie about how you need money to live and when you had money, you blew it off!" The judge calmed down and went back to her normal voice. "Mrs. Allen, do you have anything else to say?"

"No, your honor." She said.

"Miss. James?"

"Yes, I do. Here are the police reports from all the harassment calls that Mrs. Hicks made to my client. He also wrote down everything she said in their conversations." I handed the bailiff the papers.

She looked at them and was disappointed in Mia. "Mrs. Hicks, can you explain this?"

"Your honor, he wasn't going to help me with anything!" She cried.

"Mrs. Hicks, you had access to both of your accounts! Look at what you spent it on! It's coming from your bank card and the checks have your signature on them!" Mia didn't say a word and the bailiff handed her Kleenex. "Is there anything else Miss. James?"

"No, your honor."

"Where are you living now, Mrs. Hicks?"

"I'm still in the condo." Mia was still in tears.

"Okay, looking at your spending habits, your income, and your harassment calls, I'm not giving you the house." Mia cried harder. "You will keep your car and I suggest you seek counseling and anger management. The final balance in your joint account is eighty-thousand dollars. Since you blew thirty grand, you will get ten-thousand dollars. Mr. Hicks will get forty-thousand dollars." She said.

"Your honor?" Andrew called.

"Yes, Mr. Hicks."

"Mia can remain in the condo. The lease is paid for."

"Are you sure?"

"Yes ma'am."

"You're a generous man." The judge said. "Okay Mrs. Hicks, you will get the condo and your CL-Class Mercedes-

Benz. Mr. Hicks, you will keep your father's inheritance and the house but, you will have to pay Mrs. Hicks five-thousand dollars a month for six months." Mia's tears dried up when she heard that she will be getting more money. "Mr. Hicks, you will keep your Hummer H1 and the Tesla Model S. Is there anything else?"

"I'd like to go back to my maiden name." Mia said.

"No problem." The judge said, writing everything down. "Mrs. Hicks, you have forty-eight hours to get all of your things out of the house. Mr. Hicks, you also have forty-eight hours to get the rest of your things out of the condo."

"She already has." Andrew said.

"Have you?"

"Yes ma'am." Mia said.

"Okay, this is my ruling and good luck to the both of you." The judge banged her gavel. "Have a good day." Mia and Joan left the courtroom without saying a word.

Andrew gave me a big hug and thanked me. We went back to my house and relaxed. "I'm glad this is over." He said.

"Me too. Do you think she will cause anymore drama?"

"No. Her sister has a big house and Mia can get an apartment. She just wants to live the high life."

"Well, she ruined that. Are you still going to California with me tomorrow?"

"Of course!"

"We better start packing."

I stood and Andrew followed me upstairs. He stopped me and pulled me towards him. "Thank you." He said.

"No problem."

"No Dina, I'm serious. I love you."

Andrew and I are at Momma's birthday party in Newport Beach. She had a full house and she invited Uncle Ernest, who flew here with Jaz. Momma's house was pretty, and I loved the way she decorated it. She was glowing and dancing to the old school music that the deejay was playing. Uncle Ernest was swinging out with a woman who appeared to be rich by the way she was dressed. Reggie and Kel barbecued, and Patrick took a break. I helped cook as soon as we arrived this morning. I thought a lot about what Andrew said and he shocked me. I love him too. This felt real but I was skeptical because it was too soon. He's been by my side for the past few months.

Later, we sang happy birthday to Momma and had cake, and ice cream. She opened her gifts, and we all gave her a canvas portrait of the four of us. She was in tears and hung it above her fireplace. We gave her another one for her house in Texas. Everyone went back to dancing, and I went in the kitchen to get a drink. "How have you been, Dina?" Alexis asked, walking in.

Alexis looked fabulous as always in her summer ensemble. Her hair was long and wavy, and her makeup was flawless. "I've been fine. How about you?"

"Good."

"Ready to move into that big house?"

"Yes, Mom gave us a large amount of money to furnish and decorate it." She said. "By the way, Christmas will be at our new house this year."

"Thanksgiving will be at mine in Texas." Momma said, walking in, dancing. "Girls, I'm having a wonderful time. I love y'all so much."

"We love you too."

She walked back out, still dancing, and Yvette walked in. She was six months pregnant and was getting big. "Are you going to make it?"

"Girl, my feet are killing me." She said, out of breath. "I'm glad I brought my slippers."

"When are y'all going back to L.A.?" Alexis asked.

"Tomorrow evening. I need to sit down." She sat on the bar stool.

"This party turned out great."

"Yes, it did. Look at Uncle Ernest." He was swinging out with Momma.

We laughed at him and remembered him and Daddy showing each other different dance steps. "Excuse me!" A man shouted. "Can I have everyone's attention?" We walked outside to see who it was. It was Andrew. "Can I have everyone's attention, please?"

"Andrew, what are you doing?"

"Hold on, baby." He said. "I just want everyone to know how much I love this woman standing beside me." I became nervous, not knowing what to expect and people were smiling at me. I smiled back, waiting to see what Andrew was up too. "She has been there for me through thick and thin and she has helped me a lot." Andrew then turned to me, looked me in my eye, and got on one knee. My heart started racing and people gasped. I looked at my sisters and they were excited. "Dina, I love you. I didn't believe in love at first sight until I met you and I've been in love with you ever since."

I was speechless. "I love you too."

He reached in his pocket and pulled out a ring box. He opened it and I couldn't believe how big the diamond was mounted on top of the princess cut diamonds. "La'Dina James, will you marry me?" He asked.

"Yes! Yes, I'll marry you!" He placed the ring on my finger and twirled me around.

Everyone applauded and congratulated us. Now, I have a wedding to plan and finally, it's for me. After celebrating the good news, Alexis pulled me away from the crowd. "Dina, are you sure about this?" She asked. "You just met the man, and his divorce is still fresh."

"Alexis, what are you talking about?"

"Dina, Andrew is a nice guy, but he is still vulnerable. Don't you think he's moving too fast?"

I couldn't believe her. "Alexis, I'm grown. I know what I'm doing. Can you at least be happy for me?"

She stepped back. "Okay, I'm happy for you." She said. "I hope he doesn't break your heart."

To be continued...

CPSIA information can be obtained
at www.ICGtesting.com
Printed in the USA
BVHW041148290623
666558BV00006B/308

9 798889 634003